DIAMOND IN THE ROUGH

Skye Warren

HIDDEN GEM

Thank you for picking up Diamond in the Rough! If you've already read the prologue novella Hidden Gem, you can skip ahead to DIAMOND IN THE ROUGH now.

Otherwise, turn the page to start from the very beginning…

CHAPTER ONE

P EOPLE JOSTLE ME for position, but for once I stand my ground. Someone elbows me, and I elbow her back. Only a few feet of space and a velvet rope separate me from the most famous painting in the world. Mona Lisa gives her subtle, mischievous smile.

This close, I can see the crackle of old oil paint and the strokes that form her dress. I can almost imagine I'm breathing centuries-old air, remnants of the same air da Vinci breathed.

The woman who elbowed me makes a sharp sound, and then London appears next to me. My sister, my best friend. My complete opposite in every way. "Can we go?" she asks.

I link my arm in hers. "We just got here."

"No, we just got to the paintings. We've been looking at broken pieces of pyramids and marble statues of naked people for *hours.*"

"My feet still hurt from walking through seven hundred rooms yesterday."

"Um, Versailles has an entire hall of mirrors. Hello!"

That makes me snort. Mirrors probably *are* art to beautiful people. London was born with my mother's gorgeous smile and my father's charisma. "Come on. A few more hours. You know the Louvre is the only place I'm even interested in seeing."

"I don't know how you can say that when you know the Catacombs exist."

I shudder. "Tunnels made of bones?"

"Creepy, right?"

My stomach turns over. I don't know how I'm going to make it through the tour tonight. I come from a family of explorers. They want to see every sight, rarely stopping to take a deep breath before plunging into the next adventure. I'm more comfortable curled up with a good book. "I just want to stand here and look at the painting for a while. Really soak it up."

She scrunches her nose, which looks adorable. "It's so small."

"It's worth eight hundred million dollars."

Her eyes widen; then she shakes her head. "Nope, still not interesting."

"Why don't you go ahead to the Tuileries?"

Hope springs in her blue eyes. "Really? I bet I

can convince them to go."

"Text them." Our mom and dad are somewhere nearby in the museum, presumably browsing the paintings. Except they've been here many times before we were even born. More likely they've found some private corner to kiss. They're always doing gross things like that.

"Dad says keep your backpack on you at all times and your phone on."

I just roll my eyes at this, because we've been given this lecture a hundred times. My sister gives me the thumbs-up sign and disappears into the crowd.

Finally. I take a deep breath and let it out, feeling relaxed for the first time in hours. Maybe days. I love my family, but I don't really fit in. They're like butterflies flitting from flower to flower. I'm a caterpillar who decided she loved her cocoon more than wings.

The art captures my interest, but so do the people. Around me I can hear murmurs in French and Spanish and Japanese. Everyone has come to see thirty by twenty-one inches of oil.

Most people have little portable speakers that talk about each painting. A tinny voice from behind me says, "*The* Mona Lisa *is a half-length portrait of a figure believed to be the wife of*

Francesco del Giocondo, Lisa Gherardini."

Imagine your appearance being admired for hundreds of years.

Did she think it might happen? As she sat for the painting, could she imagine being immortalized? Or did she think about what was for dinner?

That's part of the allure of the painting, this wondering.

The crowd filters into the next room, leaving only a few bystanders. I make my way to the back of the hall. With it empty I can admire the painting from afar. Of course my sister was right. It *is* tiny. Why did he make it so small? Was it a question of time or economy? Was it meant for a certain place? And what was that fantasy landscape behind her?

"Do her eyes follow you?"

The question comes from someone beside me. He wears a white button-down shirt and black pants. There's something formal about his bearing. And a patch on his shirt that declares him a security guard. "No. Do they follow you?"

He quirks his lips. "No, but other people swear they do."

"The Mona Lisa effect. I remember reading about it." I glance back at the painting. "But they don't really follow you, do they? In fact it's like she's never looking at me, even when I'm standing right in front of her."

"Elusive," he murmurs. "That's the real Mona Lisa effect."

"You speak English."

"Guilty. I heard you and your sister talking."

"Oh." With his green eyes and square jaw, he's handsome. And he's already spotted my sister. Next he's probably going to ask me for her number. I've been down this road before.

"I'm going on break in a few minutes. Want to go outside for a smoke?"

My eyes widen. "Me?"

"Who else?"

"Boys are always after my sister."

He shakes his head as if to comment on the stupidity of boys. Maybe that's because he's not really a boy anymore. He's older. At least eighteen, which means he's too old for me.

I turned sixteen two months ago. My father would never let me go on a smoke break with a boy, but he's not here to ask permission.

"What's your name anyway?" he asks.

"Holly."

"I'm Elijah. Let's go."

"I don't like smoke."

Someone bumps into him, pushing him into

me. He catches me in his arms, and I can smell some kind of masculine scent. It's like he's surrounding me. "Then we won't smoke."

This close I can see the golden striations in his green eyes. "There must be a thousand girls who walk through here, who admire the Mona Lisa. Every day. Why me?"

He studies me as if seeking the answers in my plain brown eyes and plain brown hair. In my ordinary blue dress. "I saw you. I wanted you. And I take what I want. It doesn't have to be more complicated than that, Holly."

A shiver runs down my spine. "Okay."

He gives me directions to follow to get to the staff exit around the building. And he gives me a salute, faintly conspiratorial, a little mocking. Then he's gone.

For a moment I consider walking the rest of the wing, looking at paintings from the old masters. There are Botticelli frescoes somewhere here. I know before I take the first step that I'm going to follow Elijah's instructions. It's somehow beguiling, this real flesh-and-blood man who's interested in me, more so than priceless treasures.

CHAPTER TWO

I FOLLOW HIS instructions around the side of the building, passing tourists and a smattering of French. Before I reach the door he spoke of, I find him leaning against a column. He continues standing that way, as if he's holding up the entire building, even as I come to stand in front of him.

"Are you going to smoke?" I ask, feeling childish and dumb. I've never been around anyone who smokes. I hope I don't cough in some obvious way.

He shakes his head. A leather jacket covers up his white security guard shirt, making him look more dangerous. "Follow me."

Then he crosses the street, and I have to skip to keep up with him. "Where are we going?"

"I know a place."

The place turns out to be a plain concrete step that leads to an open door. A hand-painted sign above it says, *Crepes*. That's when I realize it's his break. "You must be hungry."

SKYE WARREN

"It's hard to find decent food close to the *musée*. Lots of tourist traps." This looks like the opposite of a tourist trap. There are tables crammed together, something faintly off key playing on an old speaker, and no menus in sight.

He gestures to a table and holds out the wood-and-plastic chair for me. I sit down and clasp my hands nervously on the thin red-and-white checkered tablecloth. He holds out his hand, and for a moment I have the inane thought that he's asking me to dance. That's how he looks, like some kind of courtier in a royal ball. Then I realize he's looking at my backpack.

"Oh," I say. "No. I'm good. It's really comfortable."

He looks skeptical, but he sits down across from me and kicks out his legs away from the wall.

I feel like I have to explain. "It's kind of a family rule, not to let go of my backpack while we're exploring. My dad's a little overprotective. That probably sounds silly."

"It sounds… nice, actually."

"What are you doing in Paris anyway?"

He shrugs. "Work."

"Yeah, but it seems like strange work for an American."

That earns me a small smile. "Yeah, it's strange."

My cheeks heat. "I didn't mean to imply—"

"Nah, don't worry about it. I can guard anything, so why not art? Better than being the security guard at a mall, right? And the pay is better, too."

"You're different than the other security guards."

He raises one eyebrow. "More handsome, you mean?"

I have to laugh at the brazen flirting even though it's true. The rest of the guards seem like a dour, serious lot. Meanwhile he's taking smoke breaks and asking out random girls. There's something odd about him, about his presence, but I can't put my finger on it. "Do they make you learn about the art?"

"They probably don't think I could understand it, and the truth is, I'm about that clueless. But I read the little signs when the rooms are empty."

I sigh. "That sounds so lovely, to be there when it's empty."

"It's kind of unnerving, actually."

"Is it?" Without meaning to, I eye his broad shoulders and muscular arms. He doesn't seem like someone who's afraid of anything, especially empty rooms.

He makes a face. "You can't tell anyone, but I've always been freaked out by ghosts and shit like that. They say there are multiple ghosts in the Louvre."

"Have you seen any?"

"No, but I'm glad I don't work the mummy wing," he says fervently, and I laugh.

A plump woman bustles out of the kitchen carrying two plates. She sets them in front of us with a quick burst of French. In another moment she returns with silverware.

I blink. "Do they only serve one thing?"

He laughs without a sound. "No, but the look on your face is perfect. I usually come here for lunch, and I texted for her to make two crepes instead of one."

I stick out my tongue. "I thought maybe it was an authentic French thing."

"No, even native Parisians like choices." He cuts the corner of his crepe and takes a bite. His eyes close in something like rapture, and there's a strange tightening in my body.

My stomach growls. "I guess I was hungry."

"Blueberry," he says, taking another mouthful. I wish I could be as unselfconscious as him.

Or maybe he's too hungry to care. How long is a shift at the museum? I don't know, but I've never had to work, not even part-time jobs over the summer.

I cut a piece with my fork and take a bite. I've had crepes before, of course. They're everywhere here in Paris—at the airport, in little stands scattered around the Eiffel Tower. I've even eaten one at a Michelin-starred restaurant, but it didn't compare to the simple perfection of this one. The crepe is a perfect combination of soft and crisp. The blueberries are fresh. The cream makes my own eyes roll back. "Oh my God," I moan. "You have this every day?"

When I open my eyes again, he's staring at me intently.

I force myself to swallow.

"So, Holly. What's a girl like you doing out on your own?"

"A girl like me?"

"Pretty. And young."

A flush suffuses my cheeks. "My family's around."

One eyebrow rises as if to say, *I don't see them anywhere.*

"My sister and parents went to see the gardens. They don't like to linger."

"And you do?"

"That's all I like to do, really. Take things slow. I'm too slow for them."

"Or they don't stop and appreciate what they have."

Defensiveness grows in me even though I've thought the same things about them. "They're these world travelers, okay? Other people dream of going places, but they just pack a bag and go do it. That's something to be admired."

He shrugs, looking unimpressed. "It's easy to leave places. You never have to clean up after yourself, never have to see people live and then die, never have to grieve because you're already gone. Believe me, I know the appeal."

"You don't know them."

He leans forward, green eyes intense. "Maybe not, but I know you. I know the way you watched people like you weren't one of them. Saw the way you wanted to belong."

Embarrassment clenches my chest. "Is that why you asked me out? Pity?"

"Pity." A sharp laugh. "A girl with clothes that cost as much as my rent? No, sweetheart. I don't pity you. And I asked you out because I want to kiss you."

A new awareness straightens my spine. "You

do?"

He waves his hand. "Not here."

I glance around as if there's going to be some kind of kissing booth with a sign. I've never been kissed by a boy. Whenever we go to parties together, London ends up in one of the bedrooms upstairs with a boy. I'm usually on the back porch reading a book on my phone. "Where, then?"

"Come out with me tonight?"

"What? I can't."

He shrugs. "Maybe you won't, but a smart girl like you? I bet you can."

I narrow my eyes. "Where are we gonna go?"

"Does it matter?" he counters.

And he's right. It doesn't matter. Because if I meet him, he's going to kiss me. With his pretty green eyes and his harsh mouth, his leather jacket and his work shirt.

My first kiss will happen in the most romantic city in the world.

If I can work up the nerve to lie.

CHAPTER THREE

I TEXT MY sister and meet up with the family outside the Arc de Triomphe. We grab an XL Uber back to the hotel, which is a building of apartments from the 1800s that have been converted to suites. It's a boutique hotel owned by a major conglomerate. Old-world charm meets modern-day convenience. That perfectly describes my family. They love to explore, but they don't mind the occasional tourist trap as long as it treats us well.

But they would love the hole-in-the-wall crepe shop, too. There's no way I can take them there without explaining how I found it. I'm not even sure I could find my way back.

Instead we eat in the club room, a place with plush velvet armchairs and dark paneled wood. They have spreads of food for the pre-dinner hours that include cheese and pancetta, bruschetta, fresh olive bread, and steak tartare.

Then we go upstairs to take a nap. At least,

that's the excuse that Mom and Dad give us. They hole up in their master bedroom downstairs. London and I take the narrow stairs to the second floor, which has its own small sitting area, bathroom with a claw-foot tub, and a bedroom with a queen-size bed that we share. The concierge left tiny macarons on the coffee table.

London plops down on the sofa and eats one. "These are actually good."

I sit down across from her. The chair is a little less comfortable, but with the window open I can smell the Parisian air. I open the book I'm reading on my phone, but my mind isn't on the black-and-white words. I'm distracted by memories of green eyes and burnished brown hair.

His phone number's saved as only E.

That way if my family found it, I could make up some excuse. Though I've never been good at lying. I'm supposed to call him when I can meet up. Will I do it? Maybe. Probably not.

If I did call him, if we did meet up, he might hold my hand. He might kiss me.

He might do more than kiss me.

"How far did you get?" my sister asks.

"What?" My cheeks heat, thinking about how far I want to go with a stranger I met only a few hours ago. Further than kissing, honestly.

"In the museum. Did you look at all the paintings?"

"Oh… no. That would take days. Maybe weeks."

"You didn't see any more paintings, did you?" she asks, her voice accusing.

"No, I saw—a lot of them." *Worst liar award goes to Holly.*

She makes a face. "I knew it. You just stared at *Mona Lisa* for like two hours."

"Yes," I say, relieved. "That's what I did."

She sighs. "You're hopeless. I'm going to rest up for the Catacombs."

Another shudder. The Catacombs are a perfect example of why I don't fit in with this family. The remains of more than six million people have been arranged into walls, columns, ceilings, and sculptures. And for some reason my sister's excited to see them.

I try to get into my book, which is about mermaids who are closer to piranhas than goldfish. It's a good book about their war against dragons and the atrocities committed on both sides, but my mind keeps sliding back to reality.

Whenever I think about Elijah, I feel restless. Warm. Itchy.

Is this how it feels to be turned on?

I always thought of myself as mature. That's what everyone always said to me. My parents. My teachers. Random people who saw me at the grocery store. *She's so mature!* And it's not like I'm oblivious to boys, even if they're usually oblivious to me. There are boys I think are cute. Or hot. Boys I think about kissing. Or more. Though the *more* is hazy, more of a dream.

This doesn't feel anything like a dream. It's intensely physical.

After a couple hours have passed there's a gentle knock at the door downstairs.

My mother comes up, looking refreshed. "What's up, Holly bear?"

This is a nickname it would be best if she never used in public. Especially if she were ever to meet Elijah, which she obviously won't. "Nothing. Did you have a good nap?"

Her cheeks flush. Being terrible at lying? I got that from my mother. Both my dad and my sister can lie with a straight face. They once kept a trip secret from us until we were on our way to the airport. Her flush means that she wasn't napping with Dad. "It was great."

"Mom, listen."

She sighs. "Don't start."

"It's gross."

SKYE WARREN

"You don't have to touch them."

"Why would anyone touch them? They're bones."

"Your sister's really looking forward to this. And she went with us to the Louvre. She saw the *Mona Lisa* because you wanted to."

"The *Mona Lisa* isn't made of bones."

My mother gives a slight, barely there smile. A Mona Lisa smile, actually. She's wearing a white dress that makes her look innocent, along with her wide eyes. In a lot of ways I look like her, but somehow the effect appears muted on me. "You don't want her to miss seeing it."

"Of course not. But, Mom. I'm sixteen."

The *Mona Lisa* smile disappears. "Holly."

"Nothing is going to happen."

My dad comes up the stairs and gives my mother a kiss on her forehead. He's dressed to go out in jeans and a gray T-shirt, his usual uniform. Even when other men wear suits, he shows up like this and no one dares say anything. "Nothing is going to happen where?"

Mom gives him a private look. "She wants to skip the Catacombs."

He glances at me, his eyes sharp. When I was eight years old, I begged to skip the family trip to Costa Rica. They finally gave in and let me stay with our full-time nanny. Only, the day after they left, a storm took the city by surprise. The streets flooded. Power lines went down.

Lightning struck a tree and sent it crashing through the roof. Right on top of Mrs. Brigac. She died right away, but I was trapped in a house with a dead woman for two days. My parents were frantic when they couldn't reach us. At least I was in capable hands, they hoped. Only when they arrived at the airport did they learn that I'd been removed by the cops.

Since then they've been very protective. Over-protective, even.

"I'm sixteen," I say, preparing to launch into my litany of reasons I should be trusted.

"Okay," my father says.

"I'm mature. I'm responsible. I've never once missed curfew. I make straight As, even in my AP classes, and—Oh. Wait. Seriously?"

"It's not a small thing, leaving you alone in a foreign country, but you're right about all those things. If you want to stay here in the hotel room and read a book, I think you've earned that right."

Wow. And also, what a guilt trip. Under normal circumstances I would have loved to stay in the hotel room and read a book. Nothing about meeting Elijah has been normal circumstances.

My mother looks uncertain. "You're going to keep your phone near you?"

"Yes, Mom."

"And leave your ringer on?"

"Yes, Mom."

He pulls her close. "We're only going to be a few blocks away, sunshine."

I look out the window to hide my shock and my sudden unease. The sun sets behind the Eiffel Tower, coating it in a warm purple glow. What have I gotten myself into? In an hour my family will leave for the Catacombs tour. I'll be able to call Elijah—and then what?

He's a stranger to me in every way. I don't even know his last name.

CHAPTER FOUR

THE SMALL ELEVATOR rumbles on its way down. I glance right and left when the single door slides open, nervous, half expecting my family will suddenly appear in the lobby. Even the concierge looks suspicious as I cross the marble floor. It's drizzling as I step onto the street. A valet looks at me with a question, and I shake my head. No taxi. People bustle into the restaurant of the hotel. They make a run for their Ubers. But I don't see a man in black slacks and a leather jacket. My heart hollows out. Maybe he's stood me up. Or worse, took one look at me and turned around in the opposite direction.

A black car pulls in front of me, and the window rolls down. Green eyes study me from the driver's side. "Hey," he says in his low voice that makes me blush.

I climb into the passenger seat, close the door, and we take off. He's zooming through the lanes, clearly comfortable driving in this country. A

SKYE WARREN

roundabout steals my breath, and I have to close
my eyes against the wild spin of cars. He gives a
soft laugh. "You nervous?"

"Yeah," I admit, but I'm not really talking
about his driving.

A knowing glance. "Well, I'm not going to
take you to my apartment, if that's what you're
thinking."

His apartment? My brain hadn't even gotten
that far. The kissing was hazy in my mind, the
setting even more so. Second base, third base.
Actual sex. Even the fantasies happened in a blank
space. "Where are we going?"

"You'll see. Where's your backpack? Thought
it was a family rule."

I glance down at the black leather cross-body
purse I'm wearing instead. "Yeah, well, I didn't
exactly ask permission to come here."

"What did you tell them?"

"That I was reading."

He swings through another roundabout, not
even slowing as other cars merge and slip away.
"Is that what you like to do at night?"

I glance at him, wondering if he's mocking
me. "Honestly, yeah."

"Like what?"

He seems genuinely interested, so I answer

with cautious honesty. "This book I'm into is about this mermaid queen and how she's at war with the dragons. Both sides are being vicious, so there can never really be peace."

"Vicious," he says slowly. "Vicious how?"

"Like the dragons pull the mermaids out of the water by their hair. They leave them high in the mountains so they die by the time they pull themselves back to the water."

"That's—Jesus."

"Yeah."

He pulls up in front of a restaurant. "What do the mermaids do?"

Valets come to open my door, and I step out of the car without answering the question. If I'd imagined a restaurant, it would have been another hole-in-the-wall. Someplace with paper napkins and prices on the menu. Instead this place has people in suits and high heels waiting outside, and a maître d' who raises his eyebrow at my appearance.

I'm suddenly beyond grateful that I stole from my sister's luggage. It's a dress with patches of different jewel-toned patterns with a handkerchief hem. I also took some gold strappy sandals. A little flirty for the late-night walk I thought I would be taking, but still appropriate for a fancy place. Along with the black leather purse it seems like I belong here.

"Smith," Elijah says to the man, who scans his paper with a dubious expression. Apparently he finds what he's looking for, because his brow clears. "Right this way."

I wait until we've been seated with menus, wine menus, and cocktail menus.

Then we're alone.

"Okay, how did you do this?" I demand. "I only texted you like an hour ago."

He grins. "I know someone who works here. She slipped my name in."

A girl? Jealousy turns my stomach over. Of course I have no right to be jealous. Maybe this is the way he scores his dates, with favors from old ones. I might get a call someday asking for a book recommendation so he can woo some other nerdy girl. "I'm glad I didn't wear jeans."

"You would have looked great either way."

A flush makes me turn away. Then I remember that I'm my mother's daughter. We may be shy, but we're fierce. "Is this why you really came to Paris? To romance all the girls?"

"Romance isn't why I'm here."

"Then sex?"

Surprise flashes through his emerald eyes.

"Not that, either."

My heart thumps, and I'm surprised by my own daring. "Then why spring for dinner?"

He gives a rough laugh. "Because you're a goddamn delight."

Now my cheeks really burn, way more than when he complimented my looks. "I'm a delight because I call you out?"

"That. And because you stare at *Mona Lisa* like she has the secrets of the universe. Because you defend your family even when they left you behind. Because you read books about vicious mermaids." He gives me a sharp look. "Though you never did tell me what they did to the dragons."

"I thought that part would be obvious. They lure them to their deaths on the rocky shores. Like the sirens in the *Odyssey*." A deep breath. Then a plunge. Let's see if he still finds me a delight when I'm speaking my truth. "Did you ever notice that all they did was look beautiful and sing a song? That was enough to drive the men wild. That was enough to blame the sirens."

"You think they weren't luring them on purpose?"

"There's no reason to think they are."

He nods once. "You're right."

"That's how it is with the mermaids. They'd be on a warm rock, their scales flashing in the sun. Then a dragon would fly by, see her, and swoop down. She'd dive into the water, and he'd crash from the momentum. Now who would get blamed?"

"So you're a mermaids' rights advocate?"

"I'm a fairness advocate, I guess."

"I think you're like one of those mermaids. Minding your own business in the Louvre. You can't help that your scales flash in the sun, can you? And then there I go, swooping down."

"The analogy only works if I slip into the water. If you crash into the rocks."

"Does it?" he says, raising one eyebrow.

God, his eyes are so green. "Are you? Going to crash, I mean."

"Almost definitely."

After discussing with the waitress, who's pleasantly friendly and conversant about the menu, I order the canette de barbarie, a duck cooked in honey and thyme. Elijah orders the quail, which comes with grapes and tiny onions. The star of the dinner is definitely dessert. We both get the éclairs, made from choux pastry, vanilla cremeaux, and dark chocolate with cacao nibs on top.

When the check comes, the waitress hands it directly to Elijah, but I pull out the wallet from my crossover bag. "Let me pay half."

"No." He doesn't even look up.

"Elijah."

"Holly."

"You said my clothes cost as much as your rent."

"Don't worry about it. I'm coming into some money soon. Besides, this is a date."

"People go Dutch on a date," I argue.

"Not with me, they don't."

I don't know how else to make my point, especially without hurting his pride. Maybe I like the quaintness of having the man pay for the date.

But I cringe to think about this check on a security guard salary.

This kind of place should be an anniversary dinner with a girlfriend, not a first date. At least I think so. This is actually my first date that wasn't a high-school party. The truth is I've never had to worry about money. I have cash in my purse, along with a credit card. Dad is always extra careful to make sure we each have money and identification when we travel.

When we step outside, the rain has stopped but the streets are still wet.

He leads me away from the line of people waiting for valet toward the streetlight. I glance at him curiously. "Don't we need to get your car?"

"I'll come back for it. It'll be nicer to walk with you."

My heart melts a little then. I do like the walk. Over the line of buildings I can see the top of the Eiffel Tower. It's muted in the fog left over from the rain, which makes it seem ethereal.

"I'm glad you asked me on a smoke break," I say, feeling almost shy. "Out of the thousands of girls who come through to see the *Mona Lisa* every day, I'm glad you saw me. And wanted me."

His green eyes flash in the darkness. "And took you?"

"Yes," I whisper.

"I know a diamond in the rough when I see one."

We reach an alley between two restaurants, and he pulls me into the shadows—slowly walking backward so I have plenty of time to balk. Instead I follow him, my body turning heavy and warm. I have that same itchy feeling just touching him in one place: my hand in his.

He backs me against the wall, and cold, damp brick cradles me. His body leans against me from the front, so I'm sandwiched in from the cool air.

"Hi," he murmurs, his breath hot on my forehead.

It makes me laugh a little, as if we're only just now meeting.

My lips are still curved in a smile when he kisses me. He tastes it from one end to the other, as if he can sip my happiness like the champagne I saw people drink with dinner.

As if it's just as bubbly and cool.

He pulls back, and I'm breathing hard, staring at the shine of dark green.

"Hi back," I whisper, and then I push up on my toes to kiss him more. This time he swipes my lips with his tongue. I part them, and he presses inside. His tongue rubs against mine, and I whimper into his mouth. He pulls back an inch, and my whole body leans forward as if to catch him. Maybe the mermaids did more than sun on a warm rock. Maybe they wanted the dragons to crash. It's as if something snaps. Something breaks. His control maybe, and he presses his lips against mine, hard and a little clumsy. His tongue opens my mouth forcibly, searching, searching, not able to find what he needs. Elusive, he said. The flavor of him eludes me, and I hunt for more of it with my lips. It feels like my heart is in my throat, and I ache. I ache for him to do more than kiss me. I want him to touch me, to bear me down on the dirty alleyway floor.

"Elijah," I murmur between kisses, and he answers back, "Christ. I know."

Then he stops. Air fills the space between us. The physical barrier emphasizes that we were one, only seconds ago we were one body, moving together. He puts his hands on the wall above my shoulders and hangs his head. I'm looking at the crown of his head, the glimmer of water droplets that cling to his hair.

It's pure impulse that makes me lean forward, press my nose to his scalp, and breathe deep. He smells like man and musk and some indefinable scent of Elijah.

It shouldn't be as intimate as kissing, but somehow it's even more private, more sensual, more primal, the way I've scented him.

As if he feels it too, he growls. "You don't get to steal that from me. Not without giving it back." Then he grasps my hair in his fist and brings it to his nose. He breathes in audibly, as if savoring the smell of me. His grip is rough and ungentlemanly, and it makes something tighten between my legs. He breathes in for much longer than me, muttering almost to himself as he does. "Salt. Sunshine. The goddamn ocean. Why do you smell like the ocean?"

Then he kisses me again, hard this time, without any mercy or gentleness. I don't want mercy. I don't want gentleness. He plunders my mouth, seeking from it, stealing, the way I stole his scent. He wants my secrets, and I'm helpless to grant them.

"Is it always like this?" I ask, panting.

"Never," he says, his voice still an animal grunt.

"Take me to your apartment."

He hangs his head again, and I know without him saying it that the answer's no. He asked me out, he paid for dinner, all for the privilege of a stolen kiss. "I'm taking you home."

"Is it because of my age?" It's the elephant in the room, the thing neither of us have spoken about. The fact that I'm probably underage. The fact that he's probably not. We have been careful not to share numbers, but both of us know.

"Yes. No. Hell." He laughs, unsteady. "It's because you're a virgin."

I flinch at the term. A virgin. Worse than him calling me a nerd. "I know about sex."

"You don't know the way I have sex. It's rough, Holly. It's… disrespectful. Cruel. You deserve better than that, especially for your first time."

Rough. Disrespectful. In principle I understand those words should be scary. In reality they make that knot between my legs a little tighter. "Cruel?"

"I don't even know why I wanted to kiss you. I was sure it would be boring. Bland. What's a kiss when you can fuck and fuck hard? Except I couldn't think of anything else. And this kiss, Holly. It's not like anything else. It's better than a fuck."

Better than a fuck. It's not the most poetic words a girl's ever been told, but they work for me. He seems interested. And God knows I'm becoming obsessed with green eyes and a leather jacket. "We're going to Reims tomorrow, but maybe when we get back, I can—"

"You can what? Invite me up to your room?"

I swallow hard. He knows I can't do that. "I could call you."

"I need more than that from you. I need—"

"What?" I whisper, feeling lost and seriously lacking in experience. What is it a man wants from a woman? I offered him my virginity, and he turned it down, but he seems frustrated.

"You should know better than to talk to someone like me. You should be afraid of me.

And most of all, you shouldn't trust me." He runs a hand through his hair. "I'm not making sense."

Stupid tears sting my eyes, and I force myself to lean back. He's not really scaring me, but he's definitely hurting my feelings. "Fine. I know better now. Happy?"

Gold flashes in those green eyes. He looks haunted, like the ghosts that wander the halls of the Louvre at night when everyone is gone. "No. I'm not happy. I should be, but I'm not."

CHAPTER FIVE

I TAKE THE small elevator back up to the fourth floor and let myself into the suite using the key card. Downstairs has the eating area, the wet bar, the master bedroom.

And my father, sitting at a table, nursing a drink.

Mom stands from the sofa. "Holly," she says with a warm smile. She looks soft and loving, the way she always does, even though I've clearly just broken the rules. "I knew you'd be back home safely. And at such a reasonable hour. Well before curfew."

I'm frozen in the foyer, unable to take farther steps inside. "The Catacombs?"

Mom makes a face. "You were right. The bones were gross."

Dad takes a sip of his amber drink and says nothing.

She gives me a kiss on my forehead. "Your sister's already asleep. And I'm tired. Just wanted to say good night to you. Don't go too hard on your father. He only wants you safe."

Then I'm left alone with the man who raised me, the man I trust the most, love the most—and the man who's most intimidating. Only London has ever brought men home, and they've always been terrified. He's never hurt me, never raised a hand to me. Never even yelled, but then again, I've never broken a rule. That's always been my sister's job.

I sit at the glass table across from him. "Would it help my case to point out that I did actually get home before midnight?"

He doesn't look impressed. "Curfew only applies to home. Your mom only said that so I wouldn't be furious with you."

My heart drops. "Are you? Furious?"

"Ah, Holly bear. You were my little girl. My baby. And then I come back to the hotel to find that you went out, no note, no message, nothing."

I manage not to glance at my phone. "Why didn't you call me?"

"Evie convinced me not to," he says, glancing at the bedroom door where my mother's probably getting ready for bed. *Don't be too hard on your father,* she said. As if I have the power. "She said you'd be home by curfew, and that we could trust you."

Guilt sears my insides because they can't trust me. "I'm sorry," I whisper.

"Where did you go?"

Frantically I try to think of something, but I really am a terrible liar. My mind conjures up things like *I climbed the outside of the Eiffel Tower.* Or *I went to an underground poker ring.* Not believable. Not better than the truth, either. "I went out with a boy I met at the museum."

He pauses for a moment. Nods. The action reminds me of Elijah, actually. They don't look alike, but they share a kind of decisiveness. A quiet strength. "His name?"

"Elijah." I flush as I realize I don't know his last name. I let him kiss me and considered doing more with him, without knowing his last name. He told the restaurant *Smith* but somehow I doubt that's his real name.

"Did you think what would have happened if you disappeared? If he took you to some private place, drugged you, *hurt* you? We wouldn't even have known where to look."

My stomach turns over. "I'm sorry."

"I don't want you to be scared of the world. Evie was raised that way, and it made her more vulnerable to the dangers, not less. But you also have to understand that there *are* dangers."

"My mother trusted you, and that wasn't a mistake." They met when she was on a road trip, and he worked as a trucker. It was love at first sight, and they drove together to Niagara Falls. They've told the story to me and London.

He looks grim. "Yes, it really was."

Elijah's words come back to me, and I shiver. *You should know better than to talk to someone like me. You should be afraid of me. And most of all, you shouldn't trust me.*

He sighs. "Your mother was lucky she lived, being off on her own. But she didn't have a family who loved her. Her mother put the fear of God in her, tried to keep her locked up tight. I don't want to do that to you, but I also have a need to protect you."

Shame makes my throat tight. "I really am sorry."

"I know you're getting to the age where boys will chase you—"

"This was definitely a one-time thing. Boys are always into London anyway."

"Your sister's outgoing, and boys like that. She flatters them. The unfortunate thing is that attracts a bunch of weak assholes who want her to make them feel good."

"So I make them feel bad?"

"You're yourself. And boys your age aren't usually able to appreciate that."

My cheeks flush. I remember the brightness of Elijah's eyes as he told me I was a goddamn delight. He appreciated me. And then later, in the alley, he appreciated every part of me.

"Do I even want to know how old this guy is?"

"Not that old," I say defensively. "Not like thirty or something."

Dad shakes his head. "I'm grateful you're safe, even if I did lose a few years of my life waiting up for you. Please ask me next time you want to go out. I can't promise I'll say yes, but I can promise that I'll consult with your mother before I say no."

I go over to kiss his cheek, and he pulls me in for a hug. His voice is low in my ear. "Don't you ever let a boy hurt you, Holly bear. You wait for the one who understands you. He's out there."

As I pull back, he puts out his hand.

"However," he says, "there are consequences."

London has had to turn in her phone lots of times. This is the first time I have to dig into my pocket and pull out my iPhone. It occurs to me as I place it in his palm that the worst part isn't not being able to text friends. The worst part is knowing that he doesn't trust me anymore.

When I go upstairs I shower and drag myself into bed.

It was my first date with a boy, but somehow I feel more alone than ever.

CHAPTER SIX

T HE NEXT DAY I wake up to my mother's voice calling up the stairs.

Our private tour departs at seven a.m. We're going to see the Reims Cathedral and taste genuine champagne, but I'm still dreaming about eclairs and green eyes as I drag myself to the shower. I'm back in my ordinary, boring clothes with my backpack slung over my shoulder.

We climb into the black SUV with a personal driver and tour guide sitting up front.

The guide with a strong French accent tells us about the cathedral where all but two of the French kings were crowned. "But first we will visit Veuve Clicquot for a personal tour of the unique chalkstone cellars." When my dad's not looking, he gives my sister a wink. "We'll learn about the young woman Madame Barbe Clicquot Ponsardin, who built a champagne empire."

Her eyes go wide. "A champagne empire."

He nods, looking very knowledgeable. And

interested. He's actually young enough. Eighteen? Nineteen? Maybe the same age as Elijah, but there's something more boyish about him. I suspect he and my sister will become accidentally separated from the group at some point.

There's still another hour to go on our drive, so we settle into a companionable silence, each of them on their phones. Dad and Mom cuddle on one of the seats while my sister and I lounge with our legs tangled up on the other side. We may be opposites in every way, but we're still best friends. I'm the only one phone-less, so I stare out the window.

My mother sits up a little straighter across from me. "Honey, did you see this?"

Dad glances over, still stroking her hair. "What's that?"

"The Louvre. Someone stole something."

My sister shoots up. "While we were *there?*"

Mom scans her phone. "It says they aren't sure of the time, only that it happened yesterday while the museum was open. So yes, it might have been while we were there."

"Cool," London says.

"It's all very Indiana Jones," Mom says. "Apparently the real thing was switched out with a fake, and they didn't discover it until doing rounds the next morning."

Wow. I wonder if the security guards got in trouble. Surely Elijah wouldn't get fired because he was on duty? It's not like he can watch every square inch of the museum.

Now I feel guilty for taking a break with him.

Something flutters in my stomach. Unease. Suspicion. No, it's got to be my overactive imagination. Elijah's job is to protect the art in the museum, not steal it.

My family is still discussing the theft, but I steal my sister's phone and look up an article.

The only item missing is the Regent Diamond, a 140-carat diamond owned by the French state. Its worth is estimated at €48,000,000, though it's hard to say what it could be worth on the black market. Authorities suspect the theft was funded by a collector, which will make it harder to trace, as there will be no sale.

London makes a grab for her phone, but I twist to keep it away from her.

There's evidence that this was an inside job, with multiple people working for the museum involved. The security company has yet to reveal their names.

"Holland," my dad says, using my full name in that stern voice that always makes me comply. "Give your sister's phone back to her."

Reluctantly I hand it back, then slump in my seat. I pretend to nap, but really my mind is a whir. Did Elijah play a role in some crazy diamond heist? This whole line of thought is crazy. There have got to be hundreds of people who work at the Louvre. It's a massive place.

Almost fifteen acres of priceless art.

Except I still remember the way we parted. It seemed cruel, the way he insisted I shouldn't trust him, that I should be afraid of him. Except what if he meant it another way?

I'm not happy. I should be, but I'm not.

What if he had stolen a massive diamond only hours earlier?

What if he's right now on the run?

The SUV pulls to a stop in front of a vine-yard, and my father pulls out my phone. He hands it over with a severe expression. "For emergency calls only. Leave the ringer on."

I nod, trying my best to look innocent.

It's only when I find the restroom that I can finally pull out my phone. It unlocks when I swipe my finger pad across the little sensor. No messages. My stomach sinks a little. Maybe I'd been hoping for a morning-after text from E. He might have changed his mind about seeing me again.

Or at least said a nicer goodbye.

I heard about the diamond, I type. My thumb hovers over the Send button.

There's no answer. Maybe he thinks I'm clingy. And maybe I *am* clingy. I've never gone on a real date and been kissed in Paris. These kinds of things probably end in sophisticated silence. Still, the theft is interesting enough that people would talk about it, wouldn't they?

Except, hours later, there's still no answer.

CHAPTER SEVEN

REAL CHAMPAGNE TASTES surprisingly bitter. I always expected it to be sweet.

London is two years older than me. She's sneaked glasses of wine from the bar at home. And we've both had lukewarm beer at friends' houses.

This is my first time drinking champagne, and it doesn't taste good, exactly. It's more of an experience, like jumping into the pool without properly holding your nose. The bubbles make me sneeze.

Champagne is also surprisingly strong.

I have one glass with the lunch they've put in front of me, and then I drink my sister's because she's disappeared with our tour guide. The chicken coq au vin is too mushroomy, so I don't eat.

On an empty stomach two glasses make me feel slightly outsize, as if I'm bigger than I am. My voice is a little louder than usual, my laugh a little harder. I'm having a good time, and when my mother and father exchange glances—one amused, one worried—I find it hilarious.

We get to the Reims Cathedral around four p.m.

After a tour of the inside by our guide we split up to look over the various artifacts, the tombs, and the grounds. This is the place where all but two of the French kings were coronated. I'm in the gift shop looking at a paper doll set with kings and crowns and robes. My sister's browsing the travel books with unusual concentration. She doesn't notice as I slip out the back exit and walk along the flowers. There's also a square where nobles were beheaded during the Terror.

They have a bloody history, the French.

I trail my finger along a wrought-iron fence overgrown with honeysuckle.

The fragrant yellow flowers remind me of home.

He comes from behind me in a flash of black leather. Fear spikes through my stomach as I'm pulled back into a corner of mossy stone. Green eyes appear above me, and relief rolls over me. It relaxes me even as I know what he must have done.

He slams his mouth onto mine, the kiss almost violent in its ferocity, a challenge that dares me to pull away, to flinch. I soften underneath the onslaught, letting him invade my mouth, letting him control the pace. Letting, letting, letting. Only then does he gentle.

His mouth speaks into mine, a language only my body understands. His teeth grasp my lower lip, and I whimper in a wordless plea. He bites down hard enough to make me suck in a breath. Then he soothes away the sting with his tongue.

He pulls back, breathing hard. "Hi."

A breathless laugh. "Hi back."

"Thought you might not want to see me again."

"The diamond?" I ask, glancing down at his hands as if he might produce the massive stone.

"I don't have it." He gives me a dark laugh. "How did you—"

"I didn't know. Not until you showed up here. Why did you come, anyway?"

"To say goodbye."

I stare at him, this thief, this criminal. I should be horrified by what he's done, but instead I'm faintly impressed. It's not everyone who can steal a diamond from a museum. "I got in trouble, you know. My parents were there when I got back."

"I'm sorry."

"Don't be. It was worth it. Shouldn't you leave France?"

That makes him smile. "Ah, but you assume I was ever really here."

I squeeze his shoulders, and he pushes his lower body against mine. There's a conversation our bodies are having, a different one than our words. My backpack cushions me against the wall. His body is pure hardness. "You feel real enough."

Perhaps it's the two glasses of champagne that give me courage.

Or perhaps that's just the excuse I use.

I wrap my arms around his neck and pull him down. He holds his head low enough for me to reach, but without actively kissing me. Instead he lets me press a clumsy kiss to his lips. He lets me slip my tongue out to taste his bottom lip. He lets me open my mouth against his, ardent and innocent. Letting, letting, letting. He's the one letting me consume him this time.

Then he pulls back and grasps my wrist. He pushes it against the wall. Uneven stones press against the back of my hand. Then he carefully, slowly, takes my other wrist. He pushes it against the cool stones, too. Now I'm trapped by his hands, my arms pinned beside my head. My backpack nudges against my back, pressing my breasts forward.

When he kisses me, it's completely different. Even though I hadn't been using my hands much, it feels strange to have them trapped. They're pulled back, my body exposed. He presses his hard length against me as his mouth claims mine.

He teases the entrance to my lips, the seam of them, and it feels like every sensation at once— hot and cold, pain and pleasure. As if every nerve ending has centered on that line. Then he slips his tongue into my mouth, a firm invasion, and my mouth opens. *This is what it would be like. Sex.* It would feel like him coming inside me, becoming part of me.

He finds a rhythm that makes me ache, makes my whole body clench.

Slowly he pulls back. He keeps his hands around my wrists, forming a kind of prison. I clench my fists and yank them, but he doesn't let me go. Somehow that makes it more delicious.

"How does it end?" he asks, nuzzling my cheek.

"How does what end?"

"The book. I need something to distract me from your mouth and all the ways I want to use it." He drops an almost-chaste kiss onto my lips.

"Or I'll never be able to leave."

All the ways he wants to use it?

I don't even know the possibilities.

I've heard whispers, jokes on TV that never quite made sense, but it's too far away to imagine. "I don't know. I got grounded. But it was probably a boring ending. The mermaid queen probably found some way to defeat the dragon. Instead of doing that, she would show mercy and thus prove that she was better than them all along. And there would be peace."

A soundless laugh. "That's the ending? It doesn't sound lame."

"Oh yeah. If I wrote it, it would be totally different."

"I want to know your ending."

"In my head the mermaids and the dragons, they're the same. I mean they're actually the same species. One female. One male. They live for so long they've forgotten the lore, how their children are made."

He pulls back with a question in his eyes.

"They destroy each other, you know. The dragons start, but the mermaids fight back just as fierce. They're made of the same things, after all."

"There's no happy ending in your head, is there?"

I shake my head without breaking eye contact. Those green eyes burn with hunger. "Only when the last few dragons are left, when the mermaids are scattered and hiding in the depths of the ocean, do they discover what they lost. But by then it's too late."

"Christ," he murmurs, pressing his face into my neck. It's not a sexual move. Not to kiss me or consume me. Instead he rests his head there as if seeking comfort. I hold very still so as not to disturb him. I've thought many things about my body—that it's too short or too soft. That it's too weak, but I've never realized how it can provide solace until now.

He drops my wrists, and I fold my arms around his neck, pulling him all the way in. He smells the way I remember from last night. Except now it imprints somewhere deep inside me.

This is what a man should smell like. And impossibly, this is what safety smells like.

"Holly!"

The call pulls me slowly from my languor. I blink into the sunlight, unwilling to let go.

Someone rounds the corner and comes to a hard halt. My sister. London stares with her dark eyes wide. Elijah looks up. His hands tighten on me, putting his body between us, as if he can keep me to himself or maybe protect me.

"I'll buy you a few minutes, but we're leaving," London says before disappearing.

Green eyes meet mine. "You should go," he says.

I don't bother asking about the future. There is no future between an ordinary girl who lives in the suburbs and this diamond thief who'll be on the run.

Sometimes there is no happy ending.

I try to think of something good to say. Something meaningful. *Stay safe. Remember me. Don't get caught.* Instead I speak in the language we're most fluent with. I reach up to place a small kiss on his cheek. It means that I care about him. He's a stranger to me in every single way, except the most important one—a soul recognizing another soul.

Then I turn to leave, except he stops me. His eyes are full of something dark and sad. Regret? He tugs at my backpack. Confused, I let it slip from my shoulders. He digs around inside until he pulls out a black velvet pouch. It disappears into his jacket.

Then he hands back my backpack.

I stare at it, not sure what I just saw. "Was that the diamond?"

"They search us going out the employee entrance." He sounds faintly apologetic. "Every time. I made the switch, but I couldn't have gotten it outside the museum."

"And I walked out the front door." The champagne has turned to acid in my stomach. He used me. That's what happened. He must have planted it on me from the beginning.

"I told you, Holly. I take what I want."

I spin around and run out to find my parents.

They're already by the SUV, where the tour guide is saying something about war.

"The cathedral has been threatened many times, damaged during the French Revolution and almost destroyed by the Germans during the first World War." He points a green metal statue of a figure on horseback. "Its existence today is in large part credited to Joan of Arc, who turned the tide of the Hundred Years' War."

"I'm hungry," London says.

We pile into the SUV, and I look out the back as someone in a black leather jacket with his head down emerges from the stone enclave. He puts his hands into his pockets as he blends into the crowd. I follow him with my gaze until he's gone. My fingers feel tingly even as the rest of me is numb. That's why he asked me on a smoke break: so he could sneak the diamond out.

That's why he pretended to be interested in me.

Even pity would have been better than this.

For a second I think about telling someone, but what would I even say? I had the Regent Diamond in my backpack all the time. I'm an accomplice. And I have no idea where Elijah has gone. Even when I can no longer see him, I keep looking at the space where he was. The SUV pulls into the street. I watch the mill of people— slightly to the right, in the place where I saw him last. The place where the diamond disappeared.

DIAMOND IN THE ROUGH

I'm stepping off a nine-hour flight when it happens.

A white van. A dark hood. Every woman's worst nightmare.

Now I'm trapped in an abandoned church. The man who took me says I won't be hurt. The man in the cell next to me says that's a lie. I'll fight with every ounce of strength, but there are secrets in these walls. I'll need every single one of them to survive.

CHAPTER ONE

Eight years later

I WAKE UP with my face pressed into a warm, muscular shoulder. The scruff of his jaw leaves a soft ache on my forehead. My lips feel slightly moist, as if I possibly drooled while I was asleep. Oh God. Embarrassing. Everything about this is embarrassing.

Especially the fact that I don't know this man. My hand rests on his arm, only a few inches away from his thigh. I pull back, but the belt and the arm of the seat conspire to keep me close.

"Sorry," I say, breathless. "I'm sorry."

A crooked smile with a hint of dazzling white teeth. Dear Lord, men have no business looking this handsome. Especially not on hour eight of a transatlantic flight. "I never mind sleeping with a beautiful woman. Not that I was doing much sleeping."

My cheeks burn. Is he flirting with me? *Of course he's not, Holly.*

He takes pity on me. "Now it's my turn to apologize. That was inappropriate."

I run a hand over my face. Nope, not a dream. "I think we're past inappropriate. In fact I should probably start keeping a toothbrush at your place."

That earns me a quiet laugh.

No one should look glamorous in the economy section, but the light glints off his mahogany hair. His shirtsleeves and slacks are exactly the comfortable shade of rumpled. His loafers still shine. Instead of seeming out of place among the scratchy fabric and cramped seating, he makes it seem like a stylish tableau.

People in business class would clamor to sit next to him if they could see him. Maybe he's some kind of model who the airline uses for their in-flight magazine.

In contrast I feel brittle, as if the stale air has been stripping moisture from my skin while I slept. I wipe my eyes, trying to focus. The faint scent of coffee wafts from the back of the plane.

"Well, I appreciate the use of your shoulder."

"Qu'est-ce qu'une jolie fille comme toi fait seule?"

The melody of his voice sinks into my bones. His meaning does not. The pocket dictionary I picked up at the airport taught me how to ask for the bathroom. I doubt that's what he wants from me. "Sorry," I say, sheepish. "I don't speak French."

Dark eyebrows go up. "Non? Who let you go off on this vacation without a guide?"

"It's not a vacation." I'm reluctant to share my reasons for buying the first ticket out of New York City. Then again, I did just use him as a pillow without his consent. "I'm looking for someone."

"A lucky man."

I don't correct him. My sister is neither male nor lucky.

If there's a hole, she'll fall into it. If there's a rake, she'll step on it and run straight into the pole—cartoon-style. It's almost impressive, her record for getting into scrapes.

She's a travel writer and influencer on Instagram. Her posts featuring herself standing in front of an infinity pool in a bikini with the sunset behind her get a hundred thousand likes. Interesting meals and fun places. Every so often there will be a photo of her turned away from the camera, her hand being held by whoever takes the picture, some anonymous male hand. That's the best way to describe my sister, London—always leaving.

The highlight reel never shows the side trips, the time she left her bag on the subway or got on the wrong train. We can never tell my parents about those mishaps, lest they completely lose their minds worrying about her. It's part of the sister contract.

I always keep a few thousand dollars ready to wire her and the number for the embassy of whatever country she's in. I'm always prepared for something to go wrong.

I wasn't prepared for her to go completely missing.

A flight attendant appears with a cart, serving watery coffee and an oversweet muffin on a plastic plate. I scarf both of them down because I'm starving.

I moan in relief.

My neighbor takes a sip of his coffee with a pained expression. "For this you make sex sounds? A proper cup of French coffee and some crepes. That's what you need."

This banter thing is weirdly fun. And a good distraction from the dull panic that's beat in my heart for the past few days. "Do you make sex sounds for crepes?" I ask.

"Why don't you find out? I could show you around until you meet this mystery man."

My smile fades. He's really hitting on me. What a strange twenty-four hours this has turned out to be. "That sounds lovely, and really, any other time…"

He puts a hand to his heart. "Don't explain, ma petite."

That was a lie, of course. Any other time I wouldn't be on this airplane. We never would have met. The thought gives me the courage to ask, "What's your name?"

"Adam Bisset." He says the name in that fluent accent. It's almost obscene, the way it sounds on his tongue, as if it shouldn't be spoken in front of a few hundred people, especially children.

"Holland," I say in response, though I manage to stop myself before I share my last name. He doesn't seem like the type of man with a brood of children at home. He's too movie-star handsome to imagine in a real-world setting. I don't want to take the chance.

"I'm so glad to meet you, Holland," he says with such warmth it feels real. Not just something that people say to strangers they'll never see again.

The pilot comes over the speakers. We're starting our final descent.

I make sure my seat belt is buckled, that my

tray is secured, that my seat is in its upright position. I use the plane's Wi-Fi one last time to refresh my Instagram feed. There's my sister smiling at me from two weeks ago when she was at the airport in Prague. Her destination is written into the post. *I'll see you in Paris*, it says with a string of emojis: a plane, a heart, the Eiffel Tower, heart eyes, and a few more I don't recognize.

There have been no new posts from her in those two weeks. No emails. No Facebook messages. I open the apps to check for the trillionth time, my heart dropping again to find them empty. I hope she's okay. I hope she's okay so I can kill her for making me worry like this.

And then I close my eyes, blocking out the flight attendant and the handsome man beside me. I block out everything except sensation. I'm thirty thousand feet in the air and dropping.

Is this what it feels like to fly? No, because this feels like nothing.

Or maybe that's how birds feel.

My characters would know. My readers would know. Children always know. And when I'm writing them, when I'm Holland Frank, beloved author, I can feel the world through their eyes.

CHAPTER TWO

THE AIRPORT ITSELF feels sleepy, heavy shades drooping over dark windows. Workers push large floor cleaners across a floor that's lost its gloss. Every other restaurant has bars over its entrance. Closed. Good thing I'm not hungry.

It's four a.m. The embassy opens in a few hours.

Feeling numb, I lift my phone to check my messages. The last text message from my sister came two weeks ago. It's a photo of her plane ticket to Paris, with the text, *Heading to the most romantic city in the world. Remember that boy you met?*

I responded with an emoji of me sticking out my tongue.

A few days later, I ask how she's doing. A few days after that, I demand an answer, only half-jokingly. And a few days after that, I got really worried.

A lone suitcase circles the conveyor belt. A family with two children appears with a large stuffed elephant that probably needed its own seat. A selection of individual men and women, probably business travelers. A couple who are leaning on each other. Honeymoon?

We're all too exhausted to do anything more than stare straight ahead.

There's also a text message from my mother. It's a photo of her hydrangeas, looking healthy and pink. *How are you?* she asks. *How's London? She didn't reply to my text.*

I can picture her in her quaint bungalow with cats sprawled across the patio while my dad fixes up cars in his garage. They live an idyllic life, and I know they wish my sister and I lived closer. I moved to New York City with London, where we share an apartment. I mostly live there while she explores the world and stops by every few months.

She's busy with a new guy, I say, covering for her like I always do.

What about you? How's the writing going?

I haven't been able to write a word since my sister went off the grid. *Writer's block,* I type. *I'm working on fixing it, though.*

The man from the plane doesn't show up at baggage claim. I don't know whether I'm disappointed not to see him again. He would have made small talk, and I hate small talk.

Except when it's with handsome strangers,

apparently.

Then even talking about the weather would make a little fire pitch inside my stomach.

He probably only brought a carry-on. Except he hadn't pulled one down from the overhead bins. He'd only had a leather briefcase. Strange, even for someone traveling light.

A loud buzzing sound heralds the arrival of our luggage. They slide down the chute, stacking on each other in clumps like a poorly played game of Tetris. After a full revolution of the carousel, my cornflower-blue bag appears.

I grasp it and pull, almost falling backward.

Signs lead the way through customs and border control. I'm snapped at in rapid French for not checking the right box on the form. And then I'm finally free to find the exit.

A big blue sign proclaims TAXI. I pull my luggage along the rubbery floor, eager for a breath of fresh air. A block of exhaust envelops me. The crowd of people shout and wave their arms, a stark contrast to the languor inside the airport.

These aren't travelers. That registers first.

They don't have luggage. They're wearing jackets and holding signs.

Protestors. Something about Uber. A row of yellow-and-black taxis don't appear to be moving.

A group of men surround a black Escalade, pushing, pushing, and I let out a shriek that no one hears. A window breaks, and they cheer.

"They're on strike," comes a low voice behind me, and I gasp. Adam gives me an apologetic smile. "The taxi drivers. Only a matter of time before they get violent."

I watch them rock the Escalade back and forth on its wheels. "That's not violent?"

"More violent," he amends. "It'll be hell getting out of here."

Anxiety grips my chest. "What should I do?"

He pauses, seeming almost embarrassed. "You could get a train. Or… look, I hesitate to say this. I don't want you to think I'm hitting on you. Again, that is. But I have a town car waiting. One of those things you schedule before the trip. They wait in a different lane than taxis."

Relief is a steaming cup of coffee on a terrible morning. "God, that sounds—no, I couldn't. I mean, it sounds wonderful, but I couldn't inconvenience you that way."

He nods once. Then turns, as if to walk away. Then looks back. "Where are you going? It might be on the way to where I'm going. Maybe."

Hope sparks inside me. "The embassy. The American Embassy."

A pause. He rubs a large palm across his jaw, and I can hear the scrape of his growth from here. "I believe that's in central Paris. Where I'm heading. Listen, are you in some kind of trouble? We could look for a cop around here. I'm sure we can find one."

That's what decides me, that genuine note of concern in his voice. "No, I'm not in trouble. It's my sister. She's been missing two weeks already. I have to go to the embassy."

His brown eyes soften. "I can get you to central Paris. Then you can grab the metro."

"Thank you. God." A stone smashes a window. "So much."

He takes the handle of my suitcase before I can object.

Then he's wheeling it over a bumpy sidewalk crossing. I struggle to keep up with his long strides. We round a corner, and everything becomes suddenly quieter. It's almost eerie, the way sound doesn't travel around this building. As if the riot a few yards away was a dream.

There's not a neat row of black town cars. There's only a lonely road. And a dumpster.

I do a little skip to eat up the pavement. "Are you sure this is the right way?"

"I'm sure," he calls back, not slowing for an

instant.

Nervous energy hits my body like I've run into a wall. Sparks in my chest. A thud at the base of my skull. I suck in air through a straw. I can't trust him, this Adam Bisset. That might not even be his name.

My step falters, but he has my suitcase. All my things. My clothes.

Pictures of my sister. Her birth certificate.

What if I take it from him?

What if I rip it out of his hand and run back to the cabs?

Part of me feels ridiculous for even thinking it. He's done nothing wrong. All he did was walk fast. That's not a crime. Twenty-four years of social conditioning tell me to act normal. Act nice. The persistent rat-tat-tat of my heart warns me that something is wrong.

"Excuse me? Mr. Bisset. *Adam.* Wait."

He doesn't wait. He just keeps walking, and that's when I know, when I *know* that I'm in trouble. I stop midstep. I need what's in the suitcase. How can I make my way in a foreign city without clothes? But I can't follow this man into—where? I take a step back.

The screech of a tire snaps me to attention. A white van bumps onto the curb. The man inside wears a black ski mask. Time slows to a crawl. Gravel sprays from the thick black tires. The protestors are only a dull roar. *They won't hear me if I scream.* I turn toward Adam, as if he might protect me. And for a moment, he does. He pulls me close to him, shielding me. He murmurs in my ear, "Don't fight, ma petite. It will only make this harder for you."

My eyes widen. Then something black and thick covers my head. Hands drag me toward the van, and I fight, blind and in shock, lashing out at nothing before my arms are caught behind my back. Then I'm shoved roughly into something in motion. Something hard hits my face. The floor. I'm slammed to the side. A sharp pain behind my head. And then darkness.

CHAPTER THREE

MY EYES OPEN to pitch-black.

I wait for my bedroom to come into focus. Nothing happens. This is the complete kind of darkness, the kind without even shadows. My lungs burn, as if I've been holding my breath. I gulp down damp and moldy air. I curl my fingers against stone. Faintly slick. Biting cold.

Where am I?

Memories drop into my mind like rain in a puddle. I remember the long flight and fear for my sister. I remember the man with the movie-star smile.

I remember my fear for my sister. *London, are you okay?* But I can't worry about her right now. I'm the one who needs help.

A shudder works its way through my body, lingering in aches and bruises, waking up pain as it goes. I move myself to a sitting position with a soft groan. The floor feels slightly uneven, almost like a natural rock formation. A cave or something.

I crawl forward. Something hard meets my face. My fists close around iron bars.

Not completely natural, then.

Adam Bisset. Why did he take me? Because I'm a tourist? Maybe he thought I'd have money. That's no reason to take me, only my bags.

Or maybe he recognized me as the famous children's book author. Except that the only person who could pay ransom without giving my parents a heart attack is my sister, and she's missing.

There's no other reason he would take me.

Isn't there? The soft voice inside my head knows exactly why a man would take a woman. He asked me out, didn't he? He asked to show me around the city. I said no.

He doesn't take rejection well.

The darkness closes in on me, it becomes a tactile force, squeezing my lungs. I don't want to stay here, in this pitch-black prison. I *can't* stay here. There's no oxygen. I gasp through the fist around my throat. I'm going to die here, before Adam can even touch me, and that seems almost like a gift, except that the body fights anyway. It wants to live.

The darkness closes in on me.

"Easy," comes a voice from the inky void. I choke on air. "Easy there," he says again.

"Adam," I gasp out. It's twisted that I'd actually be relieved to have him here. Anything is better than being alone right now. Even the presence of my captor.

There's quiet.

I'm not alone in the dark, though. My fists curl around iron. "Answer me."

"I'm not Adam." And he's not. He's missing the fluid accent. He says the name the American way, with harsh syllables. His voice is completely different—lower, more blunt, gravelly like the broken concrete underneath me.

"Who are you?" Was he the driver of the van? Or someone else?

"I'm no one." Shadows curl around his rough voice. His presence settles into my skin, deeper than the dust, farther than the cold. He's someone, this stranger.

The high-pitched song of a bird works its way through cracks in the rock. Why does it sing at night? Another cheerful ditty, and the realization slams into me: it's daytime. It's that dark inside.

"Let me out," I whisper. Then louder. "*Please* let me out."

"That's not up to me."

"I have money. I have some... money. How much do you want? I can get it."

"Don't." The word slices through the dark.

"I'm an—author. I have money. And my family, they'll pay a ransom."

"Money won't help you here, sweetheart. Not unless you want to be shipped back in pieces."

I swallow past a lump in my throat. "Then why did they take me?"

"Why do men usually take beautiful women?"

My heart shrinks. My lungs contract. Every part of my body feels smaller. "How do you know I'm beautiful?"

"Fishing for compliments, sweetheart?"

"No," I say, my voice hard. "I want you to turn on the light."

"We don't always get what we want."

"You're a bastard."

"Yes," he says in an agreeable tone.

"Please let me out," I whisper.

"What makes you think I have the key?"

That gives me pause. "Why wouldn't you? Are you guarding me?"

A short laugh. "No, sweetheart. I'm not guarding you."

My hands tighten around the iron bars. I squint into the darkness. No shadows emerge. It's like he's not even really here. Maybe he isn't. I could be imagining him so I feel less alone. I've never really been right in the head since the storms. "Who are you really?" My tone turns pleading. "Please tell me."

"I suppose you could call me your roommate."

Slowly I turn around. "You're locked inside with me?"

"Don't sound so horrified. I make a great roommate. I never drink milk from the carton."

"Why are you here?"

"It's a long story. Maybe I'll tell you someday. It involves diamonds. But I'm in no position to throw you on the ground and fuck you, so you can stop hyperventilating."

"I'm not—hyper—ventilating."

"Breathe, sweetheart. In and out. In. Out. What's your name?"

Pinpricks light up behind my eyes before I manage to control my breathing. This isn't a tornado ravaging our home. It isn't a tree trunk through the kitchen window. I'm not trapped in a house with a dead person. "I'm Holland."

"Your name is a country?"

I immediately feel defensive. "Lots of names are places. Brooklyn. Sydney. Even Paris."

"Those are all cities, not countries."

"You don't know. I could be named for the city of Holland. In Michigan."

A low laugh. That's when I realize he was baiting me, making me forget my circumstances long enough to breathe. "Okay, Holland, Michigan."

"You're trapped here, like me?"

"Not like you. You still have all your ribs intact. And a functioning kidney. I'm probably not going to take up space much longer than a day or two. Then you'll be rid of me."

"Oh my God." I feel along the uneven stone floor until I reach something warm and hard and alive. A shoulder. He sucks in a breath at my touch, but he doesn't stop me. Not even when I grope along his muscled arms and over his abs. Not even when I find the slickness at his back. I press my hands to my face. Metal. I smell metal. The tang of blood. Fear rattles against my chest. "You're bleeding. You're hurt."

"Don't sound so horrified," he says, his voice dry. Only faintly can I hear the stress beneath the strength. He's hurting. Maybe dying. "I figured you'd like it better here without a roommate."

"Were you shot?"

"A knife in the back. It's all very Roman."

My fingers find the gash by the crust that's formed around it. "You can't die."

"What concern."

"I'm serious. You can't. You can't die."

"Breathe," he reminds me. "Is there a particular reason you'd prefer me alive?"

The stench of death. The finality of it. "There was a storm once when I was a kid. My family took this big trip to Jamaica, but I didn't want to go. I begged them to let me stay home, so I stayed with the nanny."

"Hell."

"There was a storm. A tornado. It came out of nowhere. Whipped through the neighborhood. Decimated a few houses. Threw a tree through the window. It did so much damage, but you know the crazy thing? She died because she stumbled and fell down. She hit her head on the quartz countertops, and it was over."

"Holland."

"Except it wasn't over, because the cell phone towers were down and everything was chaos. I lived with her for two days in the house, and I can't, I just can't."

"I'll try not to die." I press his shirt against the wound as if such a feeble movement can staunch the blood. He groans in pain. "Of course you might finish me off. My God, woman."

"You need a doctor." I crawl back to the bars and bang on them with my fists. "Help. *Help.*"

A growl comes from behind me, and this time I can recognize the direction. The echo in the chamber makes it hard to figure out where sound comes from. "If you don't stop that, I'm going to gag you."

"They can't just leave you here like this."

"I prefer it to the alternative."

"Which is?"

"A quick death. I like it slow. It gives me time to contemplate all the things I've done wrong."

"Things involving rocks?" My mind flashes to years ago in Paris, with diamonds. Now there's these valuable rocks? Is everyone in France a thief?

"God no. Stealing those rocks was smart. Getting caught, that was the problem. Turns out Adam doesn't like when people steal from him."

Adam was on a plane coming back from the States. "How long have you been here?"

"Long enough."

"Help," I call out, frantic to keep this man alive. He might be a criminal. A killer. In this moment I don't care. I'd give him my kidney. I'd do anything to save him. It isn't a saintly act. I don't want him to die and leave me alone. "Help.

Someone. *Please.*"

A footstep. A creak. A shaft of light cuts through my eyelids, blinding me even as I shield myself. Through pain and shock I see an expanse of broken stone. Expensive loafers cross the floor. Someone crouches outside the bars. "You rang?" It's Adam.

"This man. He needs medical attention. He's bleeding."

Amusement. "That man would probably have raped you as soon as I put you in the cell, if he could stand up right now."

Without thought I jerk my hands away from the stranger. They're still covered in his blood. It makes him human. It makes him vulnerable, even if what Adam says is true. "You can't leave him here to die."

"Should I finish him off?" he asks, his tone grave.

"Why are you like this?"

"Maybe we can play a game. You seem to have taken a liking to North, here. What would you be willing to do for some water? He hasn't had any today. Or some bandages?"

I curl my hands into fists. The blood has already dried into a sticky, thick mass. "You are disgusting. Is this how you spend your time?

Abducting people? Killing them?"

"God no. I hardly ever abduct anyone," he says, leaving a glaring omission in the silence. This is how he spends his time. Not abducting people. Killing them.

"He's injured," I say, my voice a whisper. It's clear that he's the one who hurt this man. Or at the very least, he's friends with the people who did. "What did he do to you?"

"Nothing, ma petite. He does nothing to me. Not locked in a cage."

"Please give me the water. How long has it been?"

"How long, North? A day? Two days? A week? No, but then you would be dead."

"Fuck you," comes the roughened response.

Beneath that gravel voice there's a thread of hopelessness. It makes my bones feel cold, as if I'll never be warm again. This is a man who doesn't expect to live. What must it feel like, waiting to die? I grasp the metal bars in my fists. "A game. You said we could play a game."

A pause. Surprise skates across the air, as if he didn't expect me to agree. "Yes," he says slowly. "A game. A children's game. Do you remember? Seven minutes in heaven?"

I didn't go to parties like that. With boys and

girls. My father was strictly untrusting. He only allowed me and my sister out with many warnings and early curfews. Somehow my sister found a way to tease boys, despite a strict upbringing. That left me clueless and alone.

That doesn't mean I'm clueless now. "You want to kiss me?"

"I want to do much more than that. You're a beautiful woman, even if you are sheltered and shy. Except I don't particularly enjoy the quick sex. So now we probably won't fuck in seven minutes. We'll find some way to amuse ourselves, though."

My throat tightens. "Will you hurt me?"

He makes a sound of shock. "No, it isn't my pleasure to cause pain. I won't do anything you don't enjoy, ma petite. All you have to do is say no, and I'll stop."

"And if I say no, you put me back in this cell."

"If you say no, your prisoner gets no water. Come now, I'm no monster. You considered taking me to your hotel on the plane, didn't you? You can last seven minutes."

CHAPTER FOUR

NORTH

THE DREAM COMES to me before death.

I've seen it before. It comes to soldiers taking their last ragged breaths. They see their mothers kneeling over them in the middle of the godforsaken desert. They see a beloved wife holding their hand. I don't have a mother or a wife. So it makes sense that the angel would come in the form of a stranger.

Except my angel begs me to let her go.

"I have money. And my family, they'll pay a ransom."

I walk through the conversation as if it's a forest, touching the leaves and searching for animals beneath the foliage. She's a puzzle, this angel, but she's mine. I won't give her up to die alone.

Adam comes downstairs. *You can last seven minutes.*

That's when I know this is no strange dream.

There is a woman in the cell with me. Christ. "Don't listen to him," I tell her, my voice low. The words echo off the damp stone walls. "Don't fucking listen to a word he says."

"You don't want water?" Adam asks, taunting.

It's painful how badly I need that goddamn water bottle he's flaunting. But I have no illusions about my injuries. I'm going to die in this old French prison, and the part that pisses me off the most, the only thing that I really regret, is not taking Adam down with me. "He's fucking with you."

"I'll do it," the woman says, her voice brave and wavering at the same damn time.

I try to sit up, to stop her, to save her, but pain lashes my side. It blinds me. Ludicrous, the idea that I could save anyone in this state. "Don't trust him. God, don't let him—"

Don't let him touch you.

If he kidnapped this woman, he's going to do more than touch her.

There's a squeak as the old metal protests its use.

Shuffling. Movement. The sounds filter through my haze of pain and hunger and the never-ending knife of thirst. They filter through with a bolt of goddamn outrage.

How dare he touch her? She's my angel of death. Mine.

I shake my head against the cold concrete. No, that's the blood loss speaking. She's a real woman. Flesh and blood. And she's going to get hurt.

"Let's bring you into the light," Adam says with his flawless, fake French accent.

It's pitch-fucking-black down here, but somehow he finds a tiny shaft of light. The door is open a crack. Hope surges through me. No matter how unlikely escape, the human spirit won't give up.

The woman cries out as she stumbles over something. Her back hits the bars with a clang. And then I can actually see her face in more than monochrome shadows. The delicate bridge of her nose, the eyes wide with fear. Blue. They're blue. Her lips are a full, flawless pout, and my hope rips to shreds.

She's beautiful. Incandescent, even in this hellhole. How will she ever survive?

"There we are," Adam says, sounding very pleased with himself. He's crowding her, one arm holding the bars, the other cupping her jaw. His perfectly tailored suit was made for this moment. It could be the picture of any man flirting with his date after dinner, stealing a kiss outside the restaurant.

Except he didn't date her. He kidnapped her.

Rage gives me the strength to move from this cold slab of stone. I have to be careful, move softly. I have to use stealth, which is a problem because I'm starving and injured and half-dead. She touched me. She touched me, even though I'm just as bad as Adam—almost. She called for help. She's letting Adam stroke her neck for a sip of water.

The unfairness of it lends me consciousness. I focus on Adam's hands, the way they stroke that gentle curve again and again, each time falling lower—to the small dip at the base of her throat, to her collarbone. Soon he'll touch the tops of her breasts.

She stands there, quivering, accepting like a martyr.

How far can he go in seven minutes? Pretty fucking far.

He does something I can't see, some infinitesimal movement, some flick of his long, able fingers, and she whimpers. The sound slices through me—another knife wound. It's almost enough to stagger me, except I'm intent on my goal. His neck. I want to wrap my fists around it.

I cross the cell without making a sound.

Even so he should sense me. He normally would, but he's distracted by whatever he sees peering down her shirt. For a terrible moment I'm jealous of him. Jealous, as if I would ever take a woman by force. And then I'm on him. His eyes flash at the last minute, the final moment when I could kill him—and a knife arcs through the air. I fasten my fists around his neck, prepared to squeeze the light out of him. I don't care that he's stabbed me. Don't care, don't care. The adrenaline keeps the pain away. Except he hasn't stabbed me, after all. Instead he's put the knife at her throat.

"You bastard," I say, panting through my loss. I could kill him right now. I could suffocate him in a matter of seconds, but the knife might pierce through the woman's soft skin. That tender neck—sliced open.

Every cell in my body revolts at the idea. No.

He manages a feral smile. "How badly do you want me dead, North?"

Badly enough to kill an innocent woman? No. Of course not. Never. Except I can't quite bring myself to release him. The possibility hovers in the dank air. I could kill him. She would be— what? A casualty of war? A statistic? It's not like

Adam has better plans for her.

The difference between Adam and me shrinks to a pinpoint. I don't kill innocent women. He wouldn't hesitate. And yet here I am, contemplating, contemplating. Trying to have a moral conversation with myself with half my lungs blown out.

"Do it," Adam says, his dark eyes wild with reckless encouragement.

Maybe he would get pleasure from turning me into a monster. Even that's not enough to make me stop. I could kill this man right now, take my revenge, end this once and for all.

The woman must sense my indecision, because she quivers. I'm close enough to feel it, practically wrapped around her in my bid to reach her attacker. In fact, it's almost, almost an embrace. If you could ignore the metal bars between us. Or the knife at her throat.

"Please," she whispers.

The forlorn note in her voice reaches into some old, compassionate part of me. It's almost as if she expects me to do it. As if begging me is a mere formality, something for me to ignore. Why does she value her life so little? It makes me angry. Angry at her, angry at Adam. Most of all, angry at myself for even considering snuffing out such a delicate light.

I wrench myself back from the bars, stumbling, half-falling. I'm back on the concrete where I belong. It's over for me, but not for her. She'll have to put up with Adam's pawing. She'll have to—

There's another protesting squeak of the cell door. Then she's shoved inside, landing on top of me. I catch her, this warm, lush woman. Alive. So alive in an abandoned church that reeks of death.

Even the pain of her slight weight against my wound can't take the pleasure away.

She scrambles away from me as Adam slams the cell door closed. A turn of the key and it's locked. She's afraid of me, trapped with a man who considered killing her not seconds before.

"Seven minutes," Adam says, sounding breathless. He's still riding that endorphin high that comes from almost dying. Sometimes I think the man lives for those moments. He tosses something through the bars. A water bottle. I'm on it before I can think, a ravenous, mindless animal. I should give it to her. She'll need it soon enough. And she's the one who earned it. But I'm seconds from my own death, breathless on my own endorphin high. I have no illusions about myself. I do live for these moments.

CHAPTER FIVE

HOLLY

H E DRINKS THE water until the bottle crinkles beneath his hand. Adam's neck almost crinkled the same way—broken. He would have died in front of me. The man in the cell holds the water bottle above him for seconds; one, two, three, four, five. He's taking every last drop.

That almost makes it worth it.

Then he collapses onto the grimy floor, passed out.

I sit there until my breathing returns to normal. Then I scoot toward the man and put his head in my lap. At least it's better than the stone. Probably I shouldn't bother. I'll never forget the terror of being caught between two violent men. Never forget the certainty that I would die. But it's easier to be callous in theory. Much harder to withhold mercy in the moment. We are two broken humans right now. All we have is each other, and I can hold him while he sleeps.

I'm asleep when he finally wakes, slumped over and moving in and out of consciousness. Awareness returns to him suddenly. He moves with shocking speed for an injured man.

He flips me onto my back. I land with a thud that knocks the wind out of my lungs. He looms over me. Even in the shadows I can see that much. His eyes glitter. His white teeth are bared. And those hands, those lethal hands wrap around my throat.

"Your name," he says, his voice hard as the stone beneath me.

"Holland," I gasp out. "I'm Holland Frank."

He collapses to his side, as if all the strength spilled out of him. "Fuck," he mutters. "Sorry, angel. Sorry. Sorry. I almost killed you."

I don't know whether he's talking about just now or hours ago, but it doesn't really matter. He's sorry, and he's the only human comfort I have right now.

"You should rest," I manage to say.

"Bossy." He sounds amused. "Of course I'd have a bossy angel of death."

"A what?"

"Holland Frank. Why does that name sound familiar?"

I'm still stuck on the words *bossy angel of*

death. "I don't know."

"You do know. And you have money, you said. Who are you?"

"I'm a children's book author. Not that I'd expect you to read my books." Unless he has children. The thought of this man having children is unnerving. Unsettling. They're too innocent for the likes of him. "And I'm not an angel of death. Nor am I bossy."

"An author, huh? What's a book you wrote?"

"It's not bossy to suggest that an injured man should rest."

"Something about a fairy."

That shocks me into silence. For about a second. "Yes, a tooth fairy."

"Does it teach them to put their teeth under their pillow?"

Of course he would assume that boring, safe old me would write something mundane. My plain clothes and hair didn't even factor in. He understood how ordinary I am from talking in the dark. Only my books are not ordinary. "Not exactly."

"Where, then?" It's almost like he's teasing me, if he weren't on the brink of death. "In their dresser drawer? Should they throw it in the trash?"

"It's not an instruction manual," I say, my

voice sharper than it needs to be.

My voice is always sharper than it needs to be. I'm full of quills that prick anyone who comes near. Even strangers who are trapped with me. Being kidnapped hasn't softened me any.

I move away from him, gentle as I shift his head to the stone.

He doesn't protest when I stand and walk, arms outstretched, zombie-like toward the wall. Cold and damp touches my fingertips.

"What is it, then?" he asks.

The book. "A cautionary tale, maybe."

I feel carefully from as high as I can reach to the pebble-strewn floor. There won't magically be a window between them, but I can't stop myself from searching. Maybe there will be a hidden catch or a weakness in the brick.

Probably not, though I'm not ready to resign myself to my capture so quickly. But the existence of North dims my chances. Even injured, he's stronger than me. More capable of fighting. If this place held him inside, I have little hope of escape.

Thankfully he doesn't point that out as I shuffle along the wall.

"About brushing your teeth?" he asks.

I shake my head with a rueful smile. It's enough to make me wonder if he's deliberately distracting me. Well, maybe so. He doesn't want a hysterical woman on his hands. And I'm on that knife's edge to hysteria. I shouldn't fight a distraction. "It's not for very small children. It's young adult. Teenagers mostly. And my tooth fairy isn't... normal."

"What's your tooth fairy like?"

The stone wall ends, giving way to iron bars. I touch each joining with careful fingers. The stone has crumbled a little over time. The bars don't move an inch, though. "She lives with her family in a castle made of teeth. They're all tooth fairies, of course. It's the rule of their kind to take the discarded teeth and stay hidden from humans."

"A castle made of teeth, huh? A little macabre. I like it."

"It's a gleaming white trimmed in yellow, the plaque scrubbed away each evening."

"Okay, a lot macabre."

"Everything is made of teeth. Her bed is made of molars. Her chair, incisors. She watches the human world from her windowsill, which is also made of teeth."

"Do kids have nightmares about teeth after reading your book?"

"Some of them. But kids are tougher than you think. They already imagine things. They already fear them. Sometimes it helps to see them in black-and-white text. It proves you aren't alone."

"Okay, so what happens to this tooth fairy?"

"She's different because she's interested in humans. While they're sleeping, she pokes around their rooms, opening drawers and looking through their books."

"The way you're looking over the bars right now?"

I feel along each space, as if the answer might be contained in two square feet of air. "Like this, yes. She wants to learn about them, even though it's forbidden."

"I could save you some time and tell you there's no way out."

"I have to see for myself."

"I assumed as much."

I run my hands along the bars. They're about five inches apart. Enough to shove my whole arm through, all the way to my shoulder. No way I could fit through here, even in desperation. My ribs would have to crack. My hip bones would break. The ends of the bars slice into a wood frame that feels sturdy. Maybe if we could create fire, we could burn the edges? With no ventilation we'd probably die of smoke inhalation first.

CHAPTER SIX

NORTH

I'M STRAPPED INTO a chair, wrists bound to its arms, coarse rope cutting into my skin. My face throbs from the blows. My lungs struggle to take in air. I have one thought: at least the woman isn't here to see this. It's a surprising moment of vanity, that I would care about a stranger witnessing my pain.

After a lifetime of beatings and battles, I would have thought I'd be past that.

"Where are the diamonds?" Adam says in a singsong voice.

The fucking diamonds.

I could be done with this mission if the US government weren't greedy. I infiltrated this operation. I found out the key dates and players so that they could intercept the weapons after they were sold. That should have been the extent of my orders.

That wasn't enough. They also wanted the

DIAMOND IN THE ROUGH

diamonds that were used to purchase the guns.

Evidence, they called it. Spoils of war. That's what they actually are.

I say nothing, and Adam nods to Peter. A blow lands on my cheek, making my whole head crack. My neck bends a way it shouldn't, and I know I'll feel that later.

"You want to answer me," Adam says.

"I really don't," I manage between clenched, bloodied teeth.

He smiles, looking movie-star gorgeous. "Come now. This could be so easy for you. You tell me where the diamonds are, and I'll let you walk away."

There's no way he's letting me leave this damned church alive.

Another blow, this one to my stomach, and I cough red spittle across the floor.

"You already know," I say, wheezing.

It was a week ago. Or was it two weeks? Time bleeds together in the cell.

We were using my contacts to sell the diamonds.

One in particular, a well-known master jeweler, had verified the authenticity of them. It was the perfect time to make the switch to my fake versions, to hide the real ones from Adam. But where to put the real ones? He would have noticed a sleight of hand. He'd definitely get suspicious if I sauntered into an alleyway and switched them there.

This is the pain point of working alone—no distractions.

And then the woman appeared around a corner.

Glamorous. And familiar.

I recognized her instantly, and my first thought—to my shame, my first thought wasn't about how I could use her for the mission. My first thought was to wonder whether her sister was with her. But she was alone.

She noticed me staring. Her forehead puckered. "Do I know you?"

Confirm or deny? "Reims," I say. "Eight years ago."

She recognized me a second later. "You," she says, a slow smile dawning on her beautiful face. "You're the one who kissed my sister. The one she had a major crush on."

"That was me," I say, warmed by the mention of her.

She had a crush on me? No, she didn't even know me. Not until the end.

The sister, London, puts a hand on her hip.

"So how've you been the past eight years?"

A single moment.

A coincidence in a world of randomness.

It changed everything. Adam has always been a sucker for a beautiful woman. He couldn't help but flirt with her. It was the moment's distraction I needed. I tucked the real diamonds into her four-thousand-dollar Louis Vuitton tote.

In my palm there appeared a replica of the black velvet pouch.

Except instead of a million dollars in diamonds, there was only cubic zirconia. They would not hold up to inspection, but they could fool Adam when he took them from me. They fooled him for a few days, even. I was getting ready to sneak away, where I'd have to find the woman and her Louis Vuitton tote. That was when Adam got suspicious.

No one gets suspicious of me. I'm too good at lying.

Somehow Adam knew.

He smiles at me now, not quite hiding his frustration. I only have a few more days of torture before my body gives out. Before my heart gives up. He knows he's running out of time.

"I already know it was the girl. I even know her name. Who is she? A girlfriend? A contractor?

You've put her in danger, you know. A big fat red target on her pretty forehead."

That doesn't move me. Maybe that makes me a cold bastard, but I've been in this line of work too long to have any softness left. I clench my teeth as another blow rattles my brains.

"So, you don't care," he says, spreading his hands wide. "This is the problem, working with professionals. They do their job, but they don't have any fucking weakness."

"Thank you," I say, and another blow lands on my jaw. Fuck.

I think I lost a tooth on that one. One of the ones in the back. A molar. It kicks around inside my mouth, rubbing against my tongue, but sharp and smooth, before I spit it out. It reminds me of the tooth fairy in Holland Frank's book.

Will she come and collect this tooth from the stone floor?

Or maybe not, since it won't end up beneath any pillow.

Adam sighs. "I went through all the trouble of collecting the girl. She's no good if you don't tell me where to find the diamonds. She won't help at all—"

"Leave her out of this."

The words slip out before I can stop them,

and I immediately curse myself. No weakness. I can show no weakness. It's not only pretend. I can't have any weakness. And somehow, this random woman in my cell has become mine.

Adam gives me a terrible, knowing smile. "You like her."

No, I don't. The answer sits on my tongue, but it won't help. He already knows. I clench my teeth together, bracing for a blow that never comes. I can't afford any weaknesses. That's not only to protect the mission. It's to protect the innocent.

If I care about her, Adam will use her to get to me. He'll hurt her.

CHAPTER SEVEN
HOLLY

I WIPE HIM as gently as possible, but he still grunts in pain. There's blood all over his face and bruises down his body. Adam threw him back into the cell with some antiseptic wipes and bandages. There's something disturbing about attending to a man who's been tortured, making sure he lives long enough to be tortured again.

I've always known that I was lucky, that I was raised in a family where I had enough food and clothes and love to go around. My career writing books has paid for a comfortable life. I have a bed with a down comforter and an AC unit that actually works. I knew that I was lucky, but I never fully understood what it meant to be hungry. What it meant to be cold. What it meant to be bleeding without any access to some freaking Advil.

"We have to get you out of here," he says, sounding delirious.

"I appreciate the sentiment," I say, using the last wipe on his brow. "But we established that there's no way out. Besides, you need to get out of here more than I do."

"There's a break in the perimeter at the other end of the bars.

I stand up. "What? No, there isn't."

"It's low, in the wood between the bars and the stone. Wood's rotted."

Excitement beats heavy in my chest. I half-walk, half-crawl to the corner and brush my hands along the bars as I cross them. "I feel it. I feel it. Why didn't you tell me this yesterday?"

"There's not much space. Unless you're actually a tooth fairy, you won't fit through."

I find the rotten wood, and my heart sinks. He's right. There's even a space where the wood's fallen away completely, but it leaves only inches. Maybe a foot. I'm not actually a tooth fairy. No one could fit through here. "It's almost worse. Having hope."

"That's why I didn't tell you," he says, his voice low with regret.

"Then why tell me now?"

He groans. "It's the only way out."

He must be delirious.

I sit down against the thick wood frame, my

back against it. "The tooth fairy. One of the people on her route is a boy, a teenage boy. Old to still be putting teeth under his pillow. And he looks different. Tall but very skinny. She wonders if something is wrong with him."

"Is there? Something wrong with him?"

"Yes. He's dying."

A sharp intake of breath. "Does she talk to him?"

"One day he leaves a note under his pillow. It's a suicide note. She can't bear the thought of him trying to kill himself, so she writes him a note back. The next night he writes her another note. She writes back. There's no tooth. She shouldn't even go in his room when there's no tooth, and she definitely shouldn't be writing him notes."

There's a shuffling, and in the faintest shadows I can see him. My eyes are adjusting. It makes me wonder if I'll have night vision by the time this ends. "What do the notes say?"

"He tells her the things he wishes would happen in his life, even though he knows he'll die before any of them come true. She tells him about the things she's afraid of."

"What are you afraid of?"

"This isn't about me," I say, tears springing to my eyes.

DIAMOND IN THE ROUGH

"Fine. What's the tooth fairy afraid of?"

The young tooth fairy is afraid of being different, but that's not what I say. "She's afraid of dying in this cell. She's afraid her family will never know what happened to her." Tears stream down my cheeks. "She's afraid that you'll die first, and she'll be alone in this cell."

A shuffle and then North is beside me. He places a reassuring hand on my shoulder, and I burst into messy, pointless sobs. "Easy," he says, though he doesn't seem to expect me to stop crying. It's just what he says to soothe me, apparently. "Easy there."

He pulls me close, and I resist for only one second, two, three, before burying my face in his shoulder. Strong arms embrace me. I breathe in the scents of metal and musk. I must be smearing tears all over his bare skin. It's probably mixing with dirt and with blood, but that feels right for this place. Macabre, like he said. I cry out my fear and my anger—God, so much anger. Every woman lives in fear of that white van and that black hood. I cry for every moment I spent in fear, every self-defense class, every bottle of mace in my purse. For nothing.

"What do you wish would happen in your life?" I ask. He tells her the things he wishes would happen in his life, even though he knows he'll die before any of them come true.

"I don't wish for things."

"Ever?"

"Not often. I doubt I'll be leaving this cell alive."

"Where are we, anyway?" I ask, peering into the dark. "Some kind of prison?"

An ache strikes my heart. I miss my Keurig coffee maker and my toothbrush. Simple things. They were easy to take for granted, but I miss them now. There's a typewriter ornament that London gave me for Christmas. I hang it on the lamp on my desk year-round.

Will I ever see that glossy pink typewriter again?

"A CHURCH, ACTUALLY. It was converted to a prison during the French Revolution."

"It feels wrong to keep people in a church. I guess Adam isn't a religious type."

When my tears have slowed to a trickle, he gently pushes me aside and stands. "You know—" He sounds thoughtful. I can hear the sound of something grinding, feel the faint vibrations through the air as he pushes. "There's a solid three inches."

I swipe my cheeks. "I'm not actually a tooth fairy."

"No, but you're slender. I felt it just now. Small boned. Slim."

"I still won't fit."

"Maybe. I might be able to pull the iron. I noticed that the first time I explored here, that I could pull it out of place another few inches, but it didn't matter because I couldn't fit through."

It doesn't sound like enough, but hope blooms like wildflowers in a meadow. Irrepressible. And abundant. "Do you really think it might work?"

"Maybe." His voice comes over a faint grinding that must be him working at the wood. "And I can chip away some of this rotted stuff to make more room. It would probably hurt you. No, I won't lie. It definitely will hurt you. Might even break a rib to get out. Understand?"

"I understand," I say, almost bouncing with excitement.

"No, I don't think you do."

"It means I can get out. It means we can escape."

"Not me, sweetheart. Only you."

CHAPTER EIGHT

NORTH

HER BREATH CATCHES, and I wish I could comfort her worry away. I wish I could be the white knight to save her from this. Instead I'm the dying boy in her story.

I scrape away the rotting wood, using my hand like a bear paw. It's tearing my palm to shit, but it doesn't matter. If I can save her, maybe this whole fucking thing will be worth it. Steal some diamonds, they said. It will be easy, they said. And it was. That's the hell of it. Stealing the diamonds was easy enough. Keeping them. That's the hard part.

My head spins, and I have to force myself to remain standing.

How big does the space need to be? I put my hand on her, and she goes abruptly still, like a rabbit caught in the mouth of a wolf. I suppose that's what we are—prey and predator.

I can almost wrap my hands fully around her

waist. Not quite.

This is the thinnest space on her body. It's also the most tender. The iron will rip her soft skin. It will tear her tendons and muscles. Damage her organs.

It's her only chance of escape.

I could never have fit through this space. Even half-starved I've got leftover muscle. Big bones. The kind of body that can't fit through a hole in the wall, no matter how much it breaks.

"You ready?"

Her voice shakes. "I'm ready."

"Brave girl. You start going through. I'll push you the rest of the way."

An audible swallow. "Okay."

"Once you're out, you head up the stairs. Go left down the hallway. Down another flight of stairs. That'll take you to the back, to the entrance they don't use. Once you hit the forest, you run like the fucking wind. Don't stop for anything, understand? No matter how much it hurts."

"Up the stairs. Left down the hallway. Down the stairs. Got it."

I'm close enough to feel her breath, faint and warm on my shoulder. It's fast. She's hyping herself up. Or hyperventilating. "If you get to safety—" I force myself to stop. My eyes close.

This woman didn't ask to be involved with criminals. She sure as hell didn't ask to get locked up with me. "When you get to safety, call Liam North."

"Who's that?"

"My brother." I give her his private phone number and email address.

Her eyes go wide. "Will he be able to help you?"

"Yes." Probably not. I'm going to die in this hellhole in the north of France. At least this way my brothers will know what happened to me.

She lifts her head to look at me. I can see the reflection in her eyes. "You're lying to me."

I have no reason to stop myself. No kindness or humanity left anywhere inside. I bend my head and brush my lips against hers. It's a light kiss. Light enough that she can jerk away. Slap me. Call me an animal. Instead she freezes again, the little rabbit. She holds very still so I can do it again. And again. I nudge apart her lips. I'm covered in dirt and blood, the most elemental of things. There was nothing beautiful in this hellhole until she came. She turns away, and clean wisps of her hair tickle my cheek. I breathe in deep—smelling warmth and woman, wondering if she's the last bit of heaven I'll ever hold.

She contorts her body into almost a sitting position, squeezing her waist into the notch. I hear her suck in a breath, feel her brace herself against the pain.

It's not enough. The human body has mechanisms to protect itself. It would be like throwing herself into a fire, forcing her body through this too-small place, breaking herself to fit. That's why it's my job. I'm the one who places a gentle kiss on her forehead—before I take a good, hard hold of her shoulder and hip. And push.

A cry of pain abruptly ends.

She's halfway through, and I'm not sure she can make it all the way through. What if it's too small? What if I truly break her? Her ribs could break and shatter. They could pierce her lungs. She could die trapped in these iron bars. She could die by my hands.

I have killed a lot of people in my lifetime. Never a woman.

She sobs through the next words. "Finish it."

Taking hold of the iron, I pull with every ounce of strength. It takes more willpower to ignore the animal groan she makes. My muscles tremble with the force of keeping the iron moved even an inch. I use my other hand to push her through. She tumbles to the stone on the other side, making a keening sound. Each high-pitched note is like a knife to my stomach.

"Are you okay?" I ask, which is a stupid question. *Will you live?* I'm not sure she even knows the answer. "Holland. You're out. You have to get up now. You have to go."

There's panting from the floor. "It hurts."

I force my voice to remain even. Don't panic. At least not while she's still here. "You probably bruised a few ribs. Maybe broke them. You can still walk. Understand?"

"Yes," she whispers.

I listen to her stand and move cautiously up the stairs. A sliver of light blinds me, and then the door closes again. Shock registers first, even before recognition. That profile. Slimmed of the rounded edges of youth. Made stark from even a few hours of terror.

It's her. The girl from all those years ago.

Shock wrenches my bones. What the hell? What the hell?

She was here all along.

And now she's gone.

"Voyages sur," I whisper. "Safe travels, Holly."

How did she end up here? Except I know. Didn't I? Damn me to hell, I know how it happened. I know why it happened. And it's my fault that she was held captive.

Every second that goes by I imagine her running down the stairs, running through the forest. Running all the way to safety. Only fifteen minutes go by before Adam comes downstairs. It's still pitch-black. Too dark for him to see that she's not here.

"Hello, ma petite."

I need to distract him. "What the hell do you want with her, Bisset?"

"The same thing you want, I imagine. We're both men."

That makes me growl. "I don't force women."

"But you wouldn't need to force her, I think. That's my part in this little game."

"Jesus. I knew you were a sick fuck, but this is insane. Do you think it's going to keep a low profile, stealing diamonds and stealing women at the same time?"

"That is where you're wrong. I'm only stealing women. One woman. And you will tell me where the diamonds are. I think you resist torture very well. What if I hurt the woman instead?"

He flicks a lighter. A tiny flame dances in his dark eyes. The light illuminates the shadows of the dank, rectangular cell. The fresh rotten wood and bent iron announce her escape.

Adam mutters a curse in Russian—not French—and then he's gone.

CHAPTER NINE
HOLLY

I DON'T HAVE my shoes.

My ballet flats are navy with a pattern of small pink flowers. They would have been little protection against the forest floor, but anything would be better than this.

There's only a moment to glance back at the place where I was held captive, seeing it for the first time. I had expected something like the cathedral in Reims, maybe a little smaller, but this is more medieval. It's much simpler with a beige stone around the outside and a ring of arched windows. A square hold in the front makes it look faintly like a castle, but the spire at the top leaves no doubt as to its purpose.

Once you hit the forest, you run like the fucking wind.

Twigs cut into the soles of my feet. Blood trails through the fallen leaves. Tree bark swipes at my skin. Thorns catch pieces of my hair.

I'm leaving behind parts of myself in this forest.

There's a clear path for anyone to follow, if they want to find me. I know that, but I can't stop.

Don't stop for anything, understand?

Something skitters to the side. A rustle of leaves. The forest is very much alive, and every sound makes me want to jump and hide. That will only let them catch me faster.

Twice I thought I heard footsteps pounding behind me. Twice I looked back, only to see foliage.

No matter how much it hurts.

And it does hurt. God, it hurts.

I have the cold realization that I've never really known pain. My father would never have harmed a hair on my head. He would have killed any boy who dared to hurt me. Pain is not a paper cut or a stubbed toe. Pain is searing, roaring fire. It consumes me.

Footsteps slap the forest floor, and part of me wants to believe it will be the same. Look back, see foliage. Look back, see foliage. I don't slow down for even a second as I throw a glance behind me. And there is a man with a snarl on his face, a glint in his dark eyes. Not Adam. A stranger.

Maybe the man who drove the van. He likes the chase. The certainty spurs me on, and I gain sweet momentum through the forest.

There's a break in the trees, and I stumble over a root. My face hits the ground.

Then there's a weight on me, bearing down, dark with intent. Hands fumble at my clothes. My sensible travel clothes. Birds take flight from a bush. I fight mindlessly, lashing out, hitting nothing and everything, my fists useless against his capture.

This is it. It's going to happen right here on the forest floor.

I feel a strange gratitude that there's a grassy patch. It's almost soft.

A large hand reaches down to push my head into the grass, and I kick hard, blindly. My knee connects with something. He lets out a roar. Pain. Anger. They bleed together.

Then suddenly the weight lifts.

Air sears my lungs. I lie there stunned for a second, hearing the sounds of flesh on flesh. When I turn my head to the side, I see Adam beating the other man, his fists making meat out of his face. Blood and spit fly from the source. "Stop," I whisper. And then louder. "Stop."

Adam throws one last brutal punch before

rolling the man away from me. "He touched you."

"You touched me, too. Are you going to beat up yourself?"

He gives an uneven laugh. "You're tougher than you look, I'll give you that."

"God, I hope so." I close my eyes against the pain. "I don't look tough at all."

"Let's see." His hands are gentle as he lifts my shirt. He doesn't touch my breasts or even look at my bra. Instead he palpates my ribs—careful, careful, pausing when I suck in a breath. "Not broken," he says. "Very badly bruised. You could have died, ma petite."

"Please." I'm looking up at him, and his face is framed by sunlight. The gold circles make it look like a halo. "Let me go. Pretend you never caught me."

"There's no farmhouse for miles. If you aren't bleeding internally, you would die of starvation. It's not a pretty way to go."

"Neither is bleeding to death in a prison cell."

"I wasn't going to do that to you," he says, his voice almost reproachful.

I shiver because I'm not sure he's half-mad. "I won't tell anyone about you. I swear."

He lifts me to a sitting position, and I flinch.

His hands frame my face. "You have to trust me."

"Are you insane?" I whisper. "How can I trust you? You kidnapped me."

"Better me than someone else."

"What does that mean?"

"It means you were a target from before you got on that plane. I haven't hurt you, have I? I think I've been very careful with you. I will continue to be careful. This won't last forever."

"What did North do? Why was he hurt?"

He makes a dismissive sound. "He got in my way."

"What happens if I get in your way?"

A sharp glance. "I shouldn't tell you this."

"Tell me what?"

"It jeopardizes everything, but I can't have you getting yourself killed."

"Your concern for my safety is touching."

"I'm an Interpol agent. I got involved after a string of diamond robberies through Italy."

I stare at him as the words filter through pain and panic. "You're what?"

He glances behind him. "The other men won't be far off. I need you to keep this secret. It's important. Life or death. You hold that power over me now, Holland."

"That's crazy. I—I don't believe you."

He doesn't look particularly concerned about that. "The important thing is that you stay put in the cell and don't make trouble. I can't believe North let you escape."

"He didn't let me escape. He helped me. That's what good men do when a woman has been kidnapped and held captive in their shared prison cell."

A sharp laugh. "North is not a good man."

I feel strangely protective of him, even though it's probably true. Whether I believe Adam or not, North is clearly a criminal. Rough edges. Crude language. Questionable ethics. This sense of loyalty is completely misplaced. "You don't know him."

"I know plenty about him." A quiet laugh. "Like the fact that he killed his father. The man has balls, I give him that. Most people don't have it in them to kill their parents."

Two men burst into the clearing, and Adam stands. They look at the unmoving body beside me, bloodied and broken. Is he dead? Or just injured?

Adam gives a one-shoulder Gallic shrug. "Peter? He got in my way."

CHAPTER TEN
NORTH

THERE'S A GAME you learn to play when your parent's an abusive fuck.

It's called, it could have been worse.

Every night if I wasn't dead or dying, it wasn't as bad as it could have been. At least my brothers were with me. They sneaked food home when they could. We had a roof over our heads, however decrepit and dirty. At least I'm not sunk to the bottom of the lake like our mother. It's how you convince yourself that everything is fine. It's how you live to see another day.

That's the game I've been playing in this cell. I'm slowly bleeding out, probably infected and diseased from this hellhole. Dehydrated and dying, but it could have been worse. I could be taking someone with me. At least I'm alone.

And then this woman shows up. Holly.

It's not her fault, not her choice, but that doesn't stop me from resenting her. They're going

DIAMOND IN THE ROUGH

to hurt her, and it's going to break me. It would be bad enough if she were a stranger, but now I know who she is. Now she's someone to me.

So when they drag her downstairs and lock her up, I don't say a word.

She curls up against the wall, a small, round shadow. It reminds me of those little roly-polies. I would pick them up from the dirt, and they would curl into a ball in my palm.

"I'm sorry I didn't get a message to your brother."

The brittle shell around me cracks. "Don't worry about it, sweetheart. You should try to rest."

"I'm not sleepy."

She sounds like an adorable child. "It's night already. You've had a busy day."

"He said you killed your father."

Christ. "Adam is a bastard. Don't believe a word he says."

"And why should I believe anything you say?"

"You shouldn't." I'm the worst kind of bastard, and the only regret I have is telling Adam one night. Fresh from the theft, drunk off my ass, pulsing with recklessness. Even that shouldn't have been reason enough. Maybe because we're trapped in this godforsaken church. Who uses an old French church as their hideout? Adam Bisset, naturally.

"Did you do it? Kill him?"

I thought of the coldest, meanest, slowest way I could kill someone. Torture would have been nice. His hands strapped to a chair. My fist swinging again and again. I could have kept him in a basement over days, over weeks. I didn't have the stomach for that. My hands around his neck. A quick struggle. His eyes in shock while I told him the reason.

"Did he deserve it?"

He deserved it for beating my brothers. Liam. Josh. He deserved it for beating me. There are no words to describe what he deserved for killing my mother. For digging a hole somewhere on that godforsaken property and burying her in the lake. "Yes."

Her shadow moves until she's lying on the floor. "Are we going to die here?"

Hell. I don't know how to answer that. I could scale a fifty-foot wall or defuse an IED. But I can't tell this woman that she's going to be tortured. Can't explain that I'm supposed to watch. That I'm supposed to withhold information while she screams. "Maybe."

"This man attacked me in the woods. Adam

saved me."

Christ. She sounds almost grateful. "Did he tell you what he does for a living?"

There's a pause that makes me wonder if he did. "No."

"He deals in blood diamonds. The kind that are sold in the mall that are certified conflict-free? That's not the kind he sells."

"Then why are you working with him?" she asks, almost defiant.

"I told you I'm not a good person. And I've made mistakes. Trusting Adam is one of them. Don't make the same mistake, sweetheart."

"It doesn't matter whether I trust him or not. I'm still trapped here."

It does matter because there are worse things than hurting a body. There's harming her spirit. I don't know how the bastard managed to kidnap her and earn her trust in a short goddamn time frame, but it feels like he's done it. "Does your stomach hurt?"

"A little."

"Brave girl. I'm sure it hurts like a mother-fucker."

She lets out a surprised huff of laughter. "Yeah, I guess that's right."

"How does the story end? The one about the

tooth fairy?"

A long pause. "The only way it can."

"The boy dies."

"Yes."

Yes, she says, her voice trembling. She could lie about her stomach hurting, but she's about to cry about the death of a fictional character. She's so soft, this woman. So gentle. And the world is so goddamn sharp. She'll be ripped to shreds, and there's nothing I can do about it. "The story wasn't really about him, though. What happens to the girl?"

"She doesn't die, if that's what you're asking. She destroys her room in her grief. Teeth rain down on the city below. It risks the exposure of her world. This, the elders tell her, this is why they don't get close to the humans. They're so fragile. Only their teeth are strong."

"And this is a children's book?"

"I told you. It's mostly teenagers."

"Even so, it feels kind of depressing." Does she know that she's the human boy in the story? She's not the tooth fairy who lives with a rage so deep it feels like a physical wound. Or maybe I'm wrong about that. Maybe she's full of a beautiful, feminine rage.

"Life is depressing. One day you're writing

and drinking tea. The next day you're trapped in a dark cell with a strange man, wondering if you'll live till morning."

My throat tightens. Yes, there's rage there. Maybe even enough to keep her alive. God, I want her to stay alive. I should be willing to let her die for the mission, but more and more I'm not sure if I can. Seconds tick by while I struggle with the remnants of my morality. That tooth fairy in the story of hers wouldn't hesitate. If she could have saved the boy's life, she would have. Even if it meant exposing her world. And so I make the promise, based on the lessons in a children's book. "If there's any way for me to protect you," I say, "to save you, I will."

A soft snore is the only reply.

CHAPTER ELEVEN

HOLLY

A MONSTER WITH *sharp teeth gnashes at my side. He's eating me, and I'm sobbing, begging for someone to help me. A man stands to the side, holding the leash of the monster. He shakes his head, looking almost sad. "Who let you go off on this vacation without a guide?" he asks.*

I wake up from the dream sweaty and panting. My side throbs from where the iron cut into me. There's a tension in the dark room that tells me it's morning.

"North," I whisper, somehow needing his presence.

"I'm here." His voice is alert. And wary. Something is happening. "When they come in, don't argue with them. Don't fight. Understand? That will only make it worse."

He says this with the same urgency as he told me to run. *You run like the fucking wind. Don't stop for anything, understand? No matter how much it hurts.* Those instructions made sense. These don't. Who's coming in? Why shouldn't I fight? What will be worse?

Then the door bangs open.

Adam comes down the stairs, his step almost cheerful. "Good morning, ma petite. And hello to you, North. I had such a good time playing with you both yesterday. I think we'll all enjoy the games today, non?"

North lets out a growl. "Go fuck yourself, Bisset."

There's a sharp sound, and then a large lantern illuminates the space. Adam grins, which looks almost demonic since he's right above the light. "Don't worry, I'll give you some fun too. It's not every day I have both a man and woman at my disposal. Like two life-size dolls."

I scramble to a sitting position, tugging on my shirt, which is ripped across the front. It exposes my stomach, which has a cut from yesterday, and the lace of my bra. "What's going on?"

"I'm going to have a very good day." Adam glances at him, and for the first time I can see North alongside the shadows. A black eye mars a handsome face, along with other bruises. He wears only a dirty gray T-shirt and jeans. Muscles glisten with sweat and grime. He's coiled in the corner, looking lethal. It's like someone has captured a jaguar and put it in a cage. "North will also have a good day, though he will deny it until his final breath." He glances at me. "You won't have a very good day, I'm afraid. Seven minutes in heaven are going to become many more minutes."

I scoot back, but I'm already against the wall. "No. Please."

"Such pretty begging." Adam runs a hand through his brown curls, which look glossy and perfect even in this setting. It's such a sharp contrast, his suit in a place of ruin and despair. "I wish I could take you someplace nice. At least somewhere with a bed. You deserve that, ma petite."

"Gee, thanks," I manage, my voice dry.

"And intelligence. So lovely. You're a lucky man, North."

North lunges forward to the bars, throwing his hands through, but Adam steps back in time. "You're a dead man, Bisset. That's a goddamn promise."

"You're too late," Adam says, his dark eyes twinkling. "I've been dead a very long time. This is my own personal afterlife, where I get to play with you both. And what do you do with two dolls, a boy and a girl? You make them kiss, of course."

I glance at North, my eyes wide. He doesn't even look at me. His fists are tight on the iron, knuckles white with force. As I watch, he sways slightly, and I know it's only force of will that's keeping him standing. He's been beaten and starved before I even got here.

"You want information," North says, his voice low.

"Are you ready to give up the location? That was easier than I thought. No? I see. Then you might as well humor the madman. Kiss her, North."

"Or what?"

"Or nothing. I'm not your enemy, though you might wish I were." He holds up a bag. "Water. Food. Some medicine, even, for ma petite."

"Go. Fuck. Yourself."

Adam gives a slight smile. "A little kiss."

"No," I say, my heart pounding against my battered ribs. "Stop this."

"I am sure she's thirsty."

I know it's a sick game. I know better than to trust anything this man does or says. Interpol agent? What a bunch of bullshit. It doesn't matter.

I'm hungry and thirsty and hurting, and I'll do anything to ease the pain of that.

Even a second of reprieve is enough.

I stand and move unsteadily to North, who turns at my approach. I press myself to him, throw myself at him, and he catches me. He catches me against him, and my lips mash his. There's nothing sexy about this kiss. Nothing alluring. It's a hard, angry press. A desperate moment. I shouldn't like anything about it, but he's large and strong, and he sucks in a breath like I've stunned him. It isn't soft candlelight or rose petals, but it makes me feel powerful.

Recognition runs through me like lightning.

"Hi," I whisper as if we're meeting for the first time.

He dips his head so his lips are brushing my ear, his voice feather-soft. "Hi back."

"Elijah," the other man says in a singsong voice.

Elijah! The same person from years ago. How is he here? Why? Shock steals my breath. I'm flooded with relief and with fear. Elijah. His last name is North.

With a growl of frustration, he pushes me back against the stone wall. He kisses me with frustration, and I recognize the hard, angry edge of him. He was my first kiss. He pretended to be a security guard then. He was younger, but there is something very the same—his intensity. He uses his body to hold me against the wall, mine held in suspension, feet an inch off the ground, while his mouth uses me, explores me, rediscovers me with rough possession.

As quickly as he started, he pulls himself away. "There," he says.

"Very pretty," Adam says in that silky, dangerous way. The truth is he doesn't sound pleased. He sounds jealous, which is ridiculous considering the circumstances. "Now don't you want to touch her? I think you do. I think you want to expose her pretty tits."

Elijah gives a purely animal roar of frustration, and the hair on the back of my neck rises. "No."

"I'm thirsty," I whisper. "Please. It's okay."

His eyes flash, green even in the faint light. "It's not okay."

But he doesn't argue the point. He doesn't refuse to obey. Instead he lifts the sensible blue T-shirt I wore for the plane ride, which is now damp and dirty. My breasts are covered in a bra. He pushes it up without ceremony, without any slow sensuality, without foreplay.

This isn't about sex. It's about power, and the

man who wields it outside this prison cell. The man who laughs in a low, pleased way when Elijah pauses to stare at my breasts.

"Hell," he mutters. "This is hell."

It's not exactly the way a woman wants to be romanced. "I'll close my eyes," I whisper as if that will make it more palatable for whatever comes next.

His head descends. I feel the heat of his breath seconds before his lips glance across the upper curve of my breast. He kisses down the side and underneath. Then he presses a kiss to the tip. All of this without Adam saying a word, without him giving an order. It's as if he knew—as if he knew that seeing them would be enough to make Elijah taste them.

"Make her come," Adam says. "Make her come and you can have this."

With a groan Elijah drops his forehead to my shoulder. He pushes open my thigh, rough and almost angry. Then his hips are between my legs. The length of his cock presses up against the tender space. We're separated by my clothes, by his clothes, but it still feels like sex. He thrusts, and the head of his cock bears down on my clit. We're perfectly matched for this, and my eyes roll back. In a world of cold and hunger, this forced rutting feels impossibly good.

He thrusts again and again, but I can't come, it's too much—at least, it feels like too much until he leans down to lick my nipple, to suck it into his mouth, to gently bite down. Then I'm bucking against him, keening, choking out a wordless cry that echoes back from the dark walls.

In the moments that follow, shame suffuses my cheeks.

Elijah carefully removes himself, and I'm painfully aware that he's still hard, while I came—and came loud. I press my hands to my stomach, thinking I might vomit if there were actually any food inside. I'm clumsy as I right my clothes.

Adam holds out a bag, and I rush forward to take it. I am actually very thirsty. He holds it a foot away from the bars, and I reach through. I grasp the handles and pull, but he doesn't let go. "It won't be much longer," he murmurs. His eyes are dark and mesmerizing, but I have no idea whether he's sincere. It's like trying to trust a pool of mercury.

Then he releases the bag and leaves up the stairs.

I'm already tearing into the bag. God. This is heaven. Only yesterday I turned down trail mix when the flight attendant came by. I would do anything for the tiny plastic bag now. Instead I find two water bottles, two wrapped cylinders that look like sandwiches, and small, grocery-store packets of Advil. It's like I'm holding pure gold. Or maybe pure diamonds.

"So that's what you're doing here," I say, twisting the top off my bottle.

He takes the other one more leisurely, though he must be just as thirsty as me. More. He tosses back a sip like a shot and puts the lid back on. "What?"

"Stealing another diamond."

Sharp laughter. "You could say that."

"I am saying that. You and Adam and the other guys. You're all part of some heist, the same as last time at the Louvre. What, did the money run out? Or maybe you've been stealing things all along, never stopping."

"Why would I stop?"

"Because it's wrong?"

"You found it sexy before. You thought I was hot."

"I was young and stupid."

"Old enough to know the difference between right and wrong," he says in a taunting voice. "Old enough to invite yourself back to my apartment."

"That was before I knew you were a thief!"

"You didn't turn me in."

"How do you know? Maybe I went back to Paris and went straight to the Louvre."

"I know," he says, sounding very sure. I hate that he's right. Why didn't I tell on him? Because I found it hot. And I thought we had some kind of connection. Now it feels childish. Naive. He stole something important. Something priceless. I should have told.

"What are you stealing this time? More diamonds? An emerald? What?"

"Why should I tell you?"

"We're in a church, aren't we? Maybe it's your confessional."

A pause and I know I've surprised him. "Are you still worried I'm going to die? Going to give me my last rites? Don't worry. I'm not going to confess anything. You'd lose your shit if I did."

"Ha," I say, defiant. There's a lurking feeling of betrayal that he clearly knew who I was, but he didn't say anything. "I don't care if you die now that I know who you are."

"You have no idea who I am, sweetheart. You never did."

"That's right. I don't even know your real name."

"It's Elijah. Black-and-white on my birth certificate."

"How am I supposed to believe you?"

"You can't."

CHAPTER TWELVE

ELIJAH

I REACH FOR the sandwich, grateful that it's too dark for her to see my hand shaking. It'll be my luck that I scarf it down too quickly. When your stomach gets used to being hungry, it rejects food. If I vomit in front of her, that'll be the perfect end to this day.

"I hope they paid you well at least." Her voice still sounds sharp, and I know she feels hurt. And suspicious, like maybe I planned this. The truth is I'm suspicious too. What the fuck is she doing back in France? I don't believe in coincidences, but there's no way Adam could know that I took her out one night years ago.

"Not much," I say, because the US government pays shit.

"Then you should insist on a better cut this time."

"Maybe I tried to get a better cut and that's why the guys threw me down here."

"You mean you tried to steal from them."

"Dishonor among thieves."

"There's more to it, though. Why didn't they just kill you? And why have they put me down here with you? It's not just because it's a convenient prison, is it? There's a reason."

She's smart. Too fucking smart. "I think Adam wants us to get close."

"I figured that when he asked us to kiss. Why?"

That makes me pause. I'm a cold bastard, but I don't want to tell a woman she'll be tortured. Because I showed weakness. This is what happens when I care about someone. They get hurt. "What happened when he found you?" I ask instead of answering.

"He saved me. And he told me he was an Interpol agent undercover. That he'd try to keep me safe if he could. So maybe he has backup nearby or something."

Hell. I hadn't expected Adam to come clean about that. "He's an Interpol agent, all right. One who's on the take. That's his part in this job, to clear the way with the authorities."

A pause. "You could be wrong though, right? He could have told you he'd help you, but in reality he's planning to turn all of you in."

"That's not going to happen."

"What is going to happen, then?"

"He's going to make us—do things. Until he feels like I'm invested enough in you as a human being. And then he'll torture you. Because I have information that he wants." I try to keep my words uneven, free of the anger and anguish they're causing me. It will be much worse for her. It's always worse for the woman.

She's silent a long moment. This woman read about vicious mermaids and dragons committing war crimes. She wrote about a rebellious tooth fairy and a dying boy. She knows what kind of torture might happen here. And she knows how this ends.

Finally she says, "Are you sure about Adam?"

It's a loaded question, but I don't tell her that. "He's not a good guy."

A longer pause this time. "What are we going to do about it?"

I finish the last bite of the sandwich and toss away the paper. If I get hungry enough in a few days, I might need to eat that, too. Then again, I don't think this will last that long. "What are we going to do about what?"

"Escape."

"You think we're going to escape?"

"Well, it's either that or some sort of murder-suicide plan, but either way Adam's not going to get the information he wants, is he? So let's plan an escape."

My breath catches at the impossible bravery of this woman. "I'd think you'd be begging me to tell him whatever he wants to know. The location of some diamonds, maybe."

"You aren't going to tell him."

"No," I say slowly. "I won't tell him what he wants to know."

Even if he tortured her in front of me. Even if it absolutely kills me to watch. The knowledge sits like acid inside me. It would feel so good to give it to someone else.

"Then we have to escape," she says, her voice flat, devoid of surprise, as if she had no right to expect human decency from me. "As soon as possible."

"I'm not saying no, sweetheart." I shift on the cold concrete, feeling like an extreme bastard. "And normally I'm not one to complain, but I should point out that I have big bones unlikely to fit into small places. Even though about five of them are broken right now."

"Then we'll go out the door."

"How do you propose we do that?"

"We'll think of something cunning. You're the thief. You should be good at that."

God. Every time she calls me a thief, I want to kiss her. I want to pin her to the floor and fuck her, especially since I found out she's Holly. "What's with the name?"

"What?"

"Holland."

There's a weighted pause. "It's just a name."

"Is it your real name? Or your pen name?"

"It's my real name."

"There's more to this story."

"What does it matter? I'm trapped by a man you won't even tell me about." Her frustration zips through the air like electricity, lighting me up from the inside out. I don't want to be too weak for this, too weak to protect her, but it was not a goddamn game—not really.

"I'll tell you how I ended up in here. You tell me about your name. Fair?"

A pause. "Fair."

I lean my head back until it hits a shallow puddle. Christ. "It's my job to stop this operation. It's also my job to steal from it. So I did my job."

"What kind of boss asks you to do that?"

The US government. "Not a very ethical one. So the other guys jump me. Five on one makes for some ugly bruises. I ended up in here, and shortly after that, you came in."

That isn't quite the whole story. Adam left me here with those bastards. One of them in particular, Peter, has a really nasty streak. I have the cigar burns and whip marks to prove it. Between the beatings, the torture, and the starvation, I'm weak as a kitten.

The truly interesting part, though, is that Adam was only gone for a full day. Around twenty-four hours. Barely enough time to fly to the States and then back. He probably didn't even leave the airport there. Why? He's so mercurial that it could be anything. Maybe he fancied a fuck with a flight attendant. Or maybe he had a hankering for plane food. Either way, he came back with this woman. Holland, she said her name was. Holland Frank.

"Fine," she says on a long sigh. "Holland is my real name, but I only use it for legal documents. And for my books. It's an awkward name that everyone asks me about."

"Your parents like tulips?"

"Exhibit A."

"Or was it some kind of commentary about tilting at windmills."

"I think then my name would have been

Spain."

"And why Holland? I think Netherlands has more of a ring to it."

"Are you done yet?"

"This is my only entertainment. I could literally go all night."

"Since you insist on knowing, and you did hold up your end up the bargain, I'll tell you. My parents named me Holland because that's where I was conceived."

"And your sister?"

"London."

"Wow. That's kind of sweet. Until you think about it."

"Exactly. It is kind of sweet until you realize it's about where your parents had sex."

"And then you just walk around like a sex souvenir."

"Aren't all kids sex souvenirs really?"

"Yeah, but they aren't all labeled with the city's name."

"So that's why I go by Holly."

"And your pen name?"

"They wanted me to use a male pen name. Or something ambiguous like H.D. Frank. Male pen names tend to sell better, for the same exact book."

"So you went with Holland."

"It's not really a girl's name. Imagine if I'd been conceived in Antarctica."

"They wouldn't have done that to you. Would they?"

"They love me, but they are really into the meaning of things."

"Portugal? Britain?"

"I'm sure they would be fair game." She doesn't sound mad about it, though. She sounds wistful, as if she loves her family. As if she misses them. That's one upside to having a bastard of a father. I could be tortured for years and never miss him for a second.

"My father was a cruel bastard, and even he wouldn't name me Madagascar." Not that he'd actually been to Madagascar or anywhere interesting. He would have had to call me Podunk, along with both my brothers, because that's where we were conceived.

Her attention turns softer, more interested. "He was cruel?"

"There were three of us. Three brothers. I was the youngest, which means I was the one left behind when they enlisted." Memories are black as night. "To say he was cruel is to call this cell cold. It can't come close to describing the bone-deep chill."

"I'm sorry," she says softly. "I can't imagine."

"That's a good thing. No one should know what it's like."

"I love my sister. We fought like crazy and then we would hug and go to sleep in the same bed; even when we were ten years old, we slept on the same twin bed. No matter what my parents did, they couldn't get us to sleep in separate rooms. Until she discovered boys."

"Your parents," I ask gingerly. "Are they alive?"

"Oh yes." Her voice turns soft. "Very much alive and well. After traveling the world, they settled in northern New York. Every other weekend they drive to Niagara Falls."

"Do they know where you are?" It's both a good and bad thing if they do.

"No," she says. "My sister and I have a long-standing pact, going all the way from when we were little. We don't tattle on the other one. We don't get each other in trouble. We don't make our parents worry if we don't have to. For example, London never told them she found me with a boy outside the cathedral in Reims."

I have this sudden memory, this recollection of tasting her.

You don't know the way I have sex. It's rough, Holly. It's... disrespectful. Cruel. You deserve better than that, especially for your first time.

I'm embarrassed that I told her that. She was so innocent. Too innocent for me to even touch. What the fuck had I been thinking? I hope she found some kind, gentle person to take her virginity. Someone who would whisper sweet words and hold her afterward.

"He was cruel," I say, though that's an understatement.

It's hard to explain for someone with loving, if quirky, parents. They can never fully understand what it's like to know fear before you know love.

"I'm sorry," she whispers. "Is that why you killed him?"

I was beaten and burned and battered to within an inch of death, but it didn't hurt as much as the memory. Searing pain through my body that no amount of fighting or fucking ever really remove. I keep thinking that one more job will make me forget, but it won't.

Soft hands move gently over my arm, my side, noting when I stiffen. She curls herself into the side of my chest like a cat seeking warmth. Or offering warmth. Her head rests on my shoulder. With shock I realize this is how it would have been—if I had fucked her eight years ago, if I had held her afterward. This many years later, we're having that moment of intimacy I'd been too afraid to take. And why? Maybe I shouldn't have pushed her away. What would have happened if I'd told her everything about the Louvre and the diamond?

It makes me want to test the waters here, in a place that couldn't possibly end in a happy way. A church that has seen its share of death and pain already.

"I watched him kill my mother. He assumed I was too young to understand. Or remember."

"Oh my God," she says, burying her head deeper into my shoulder. It hurts, but I don't tell her to stop. It also feels good. That pretty much defines my feelings for her.

Being near her is heaven and hell.

"You don't have to tell me," she says, her voice mournful.

I've never had anyone mourn me before. "She sang to me. I remember that. Only when he wasn't around. But he came home early one day, or something happened. They were fighting. He pushed her. She hit her head. He dragged her body out of the house by her feet."

"Did the police question you?"

"I was three."

"Oh God. Elijah." And then more softly. "Is that your real name?"

"Yes. I used my real name on my first mission only." I would tell her anything in this moment. My full name. My social security number. My rank. My mission. She doesn't know the power she holds over me. I would jeopardize an entire military operation because she smells so sweet. That's the terrible part of being a man who cares about a woman. It makes him weak.

"And you remember?"

"Oh, I remembered. I remembered the way he packed her luggage and buried that, too. My brothers always thought she ran away. That she got fed up with the beatings and left, but she never would have left us behind."

"I'm so sorry. What a terrible burden for you to carry."

"I told him before I killed him. I told him what I knew. It didn't have anything to do with all the times he backhanded me or all the nights I went hungry. It was for her."

"Elijah, no matter what you think—he didn't break you."

How does she know? How does she know my secret fear?

Except she's wrong, of course. I broke when I was three years old and saw my mother's lifeless eyes staring at me. After that I became only a being with one purpose.

Every breath, every step had one goal.

To become strong enough to get revenge.

I kiss the crown of her head because I don't want to ruin the ferocity of hope in her voice. It's enough to let her believe there's kindness inside me a little while longer.

We fall asleep to the sound of a distant drip, the sun moving over us, unseen and unfelt, taking warmth only from each other.

CHAPTER THIRTEEN

ELIJAH

THE NEXT EVENING Adam comes downstairs holding a lamp and what looks like a picnic basket. It's made of wicker and appears heavy by the way he's holding it. More valuable than gold, if there's cheese and bread inside. My empty stomach claws itself from the inside.

He sets down the basket and sits on top of the flat surface it creates, crossing his legs in the way only elegant European men can do. "We had a good time yesterday, non?"

I lunge at him through the bars. Even knowing I'm going to be caught by iron against my throat, it doesn't hold me back. I throw myself into the attack, growling, snarling, becoming feral in my desire to kick his ass. The torture isn't cigar burns and whips.

The torture is becoming close to this woman.

Adam makes a tsk sound. "That's no way to treat a woman. You made her come, yes, but you were cold. Not tender. She felt embarrassed, didn't she?"

I don't have to look behind me to know she's blushing. "Of course she's fucking embarrassed. You forced me to touch her."

"Forced? Such language. I didn't force you to do anything."

"Then hand over that fucking basket."

"In a moment," he says, humming to himself in a way that's both psychotic and happy. "First I would like to see you make her come, more soft this time. More loving."

"I don't love her."

A sharp look from Adam. "She can hear you."

"I will rip your fucking throat out."

It's to his credit that he looks uneasy, as if he knows how seriously I mean that threat. Then he brightens. "I brought you some gifts. There is no better dessert than French patisserie. The tarte tatin, the mille-feuille, and the eclairs."

I have a sudden memory of eating eclairs with a young Holly.

She comes to stand beside me, her chin high. "We don't want it, Paul Hollywood."

I'm forced to face how thin her arms look, how slender her frame. She needs this food, no matter how I feel about it. No matter how much I resent being forced to violate her. Which is worse—touching her without consent or letting her starve? It's a devil's choice.

Adam pulls out a pistol. "Then we'll see how much you enjoy fucking a corpse."

In a flash I'm standing in front of Holly, blocking her from his bullet. It won't do any good, this protection of her, because I have no weapon. A bullet could rip through my skin and slam into hers. She would be injured. Maybe killed. The idea makes me sick.

"I'll play your game," I bite out.

He smiles. "I thought you might change your mind."

I wait until he puts the pistol back into his jacket pocket before turning to face Holly. Standing this way, her face is in shadow. I'm sure mine is, too. Neither of us can clearly see the other, but we're intimate. Close.

My whisper can only be heard by her. "Are you ready?"

She whispers, "No."

I don't know why I asked. There isn't any time. There isn't any choice. I take a step toward her, and she doesn't back away. I'm tempted to throw her to the stone floor and fuck her. It's the wrong impulse at a time like this. I should be reluctant.

Not an eager participant.

My hard cock proves that I'm twisted inside.

Her face is in shadow, but the rest of her is finally visible after so long in the darkness. After so long in my memory. She's wearing blue leggings and a slightly darker blue tunic that feel like grown-up versions of the blue dress she wore to the museum. They're both smudged with dirt and grime, the shirt torn in a way that makes my stomach clench.

She was attacked when she tried to escape. Hurt.

And I'm here to do it again.

"Be gentle with her," Adam says in a taunting voice.

And the worst part is, he's right. I do need to be gentle with her. I do need to be loving. I make my touch an apology as I stroke her temple with the backs of my fingers. She leans into my hand, and I coax her again and again until she's pressing her cheek to my palm like a cat.

Last time he only had a match to light the space, and the minimal light from the open door at the top of the stairs. This time, with a lantern, I can see her breasts clearly as I lift the tunic. I can watch as her skin turns tight with goose bumps, as her nipples turn to hard pebbles. I bend down to taste one. Even in this hellhole she tastes sweet. Beneath the dirt and the sweat, I taste the elemental essence of woman. I taste Holly. My mind remembers her as clearly as it does the dark chocolate in the eclair. Forbidden temptation. Indulgence. Regret.

I slide my palm down her stomach, beneath the waistband of her leggings, to the place that's already wet for me. Or is it wet for Adam? That's the most fucked part of all—that he's the one actually orchestrating this. You can fuck a woman with your cock, or a dildo, or a goddamn beer bottle. Adam Bisset? He's fucking her through me.

"How does she feel?" he says, his voice low, and I realize he's turned on.

I've never been the kind of guy who was afraid of other men in the locker room. I grew up with brothers and then joined the military. I'm not homophobic, but it's still disconcerting to realize there's an aroused male in the room while I'm finger fucking a woman.

My first threesome is happening, and it's against my will.

"She feels like fucking pussy," I grit out.

"Tell me more," he says, a warning in his

voice.

"Hot. Wet. She's fucking swollen. Is that what you want to hear? She feels like she'd be heaven around my cock. She feels like a goddamn dream."

My thumb brushes her clit, and she comes on the final word, squeezing my fingers, gushing her arousal onto my fingers, crying out my name.

Elijah. Not Adam. And sick as this is, it feels like a triumph.

CHAPTER FOURTEEN

HOLLY

FOOTSTEPS COMING DOWN the stairs.

It's the next morning, and I scramble to get up, but Elijah doesn't move—not even when I jostle him to stand. He won't want to be caught unawares.

He won't want to be lying down to face Adam.

A match strikes.

Except it isn't Adam who comes down the stairs. It's the man from the forest, the one who held me down. Peter. His face looks less swollen now. There's a white bandage covering one eye. Adam did that damage. He beat the man for hurting me.

From the look in one dark eye, he's here for revenge.

Elijah doesn't move. Not an inch. Terror jams my heart. What if his heart stopped beating during the night? Was he cold, even as I held him? Is he dead?

And then I realize—no, he's playing dead.

This is the plan for escape, the improvisation that's our last bid for survival. "Please," I say, running to the gate. "You have to help him. He won't wake up."

A sigh. He sounds genuinely sad. "I wanted to be the one to kill him."

"He can't be dead." My voice is rising, turning supersonic. "Please, you have to do something for him. Get a doctor. Help him. Something."

Peter cracks his knuckles. He tilts his head until there's a sound, and then tilts it the other way. It's like he's gearing up for a workout. "Adam doesn't have the stomach for this work. Thinks you can sell guns without hurting anyone."

My blood runs cold. I assumed they were trying to steal something. More diamonds, probably. Some other kinds of art, at a stretch. Selling guns? That's something else entirely.

"And that kind of weakness, it can make you hesitate. Someone like me, I don't hesitate. You know why that is, pretty girl?"

My stomach crawls. "No. Don't. I want Adam. Get Adam."

"Because I like to hurt people."

Peter opens the gate, and I have the sick realization that Elijah wasn't pretending to play dead. He's actually dead on the floor a few feet behind me. He doesn't move even as the man stalks into the cell. I back up, tripping over him by accident. I scramble up from his cooling body in horror. Everything has turned upside down. Elijah isn't going to help. I'm all alone again, all alone with a tree through the roof and a storm raging outside. There's no one else.

This storm has a single dark eye and hard muscles.

He holds up the match between us as it burns to his fingers. Then darkness.

He's on me in a second, before I can suck in a breath, before I can scream. His weight buries me, and I struggle against an avalanche of dirt. I can't move or breathe. My kicks and punches are useless, useless, useless. He grasps my breast and twists, and I cry out.

Alone. I'm alone with the dead and dying. It's my greatest fear, my secret horror, and I lash out, a wild woman, dangerous and strengthened from pure rage.

I reach into his right eye, claw it with my fingers and feel something warm and wet.

He screams in my ear, and I kick him again.

His weight falls away from me, and there's a sickening thud. Then another one. Another. In a sort of dazed confusion I sit up and scoot away from the terrifying sounds.

There's a sharp crack.

"Are you okay?" Elijah's voice comes from the dark.

"Oh God. I thought you had really died."

"But you improvised so quickly."

"Well, first I thought it was a ruse." My voice is coming far too fast, my tongue tripping over the syllables. "And then you didn't move, you felt so cold, you didn't get up."

Sobs wrench out of my chest, and in a second he has me trapped against him, his hand covering my mouth. "Not yet," he says, his voice low. "Hold it in a little longer."

My eyes wide, I nod against his hand.

He slowly releases me. "Come on. We have to go before Adam comes looking."

Escape. It's what I asked of him, this impossible task. And he's done it. It feels a little bit like a dream when he leads me through the open cell door. As if I might wake up again, this time to discover that we're both still trapped behind bars.

Or worse—wake up to find the man's weight suffocating me.

The bright flare of the lantern. Adam.

He smiles, holding that damned pistol. "We're ready to begin."

"What do you mean?" I ask, my voice shaking.

"I wasn't sure whether Elijah had really bonded to you, whether you meant something or you were just another pussy. He would not usually hesitate to put a woman into the line of fire, would he?" Without waiting for an answer, he says, "But you're different."

"I'm not different," I say because I'm the boring one. The plain one. The one who looks dull and flat behind my gorgeous sister. Elijah hadn't looked at her all those years ago. He looked at me, but that was only because he needed someone convenient to steal the diamond.

"Ah, ma petite," Adam says, shaking his head sadly. "You are more beautiful than you know. But you won't be for very long. I'm afraid that's the only way this works. I must hurt you to get the information I need."

"Bastard," Elijah mutters from behind me.

He sounds pissed but not... especially concerned. As if he knows the torture is about to happen. As if it's unstoppable. My insides grow cold. "Please," I whisper. "No."

"You beg so pretty," Adam says, looking regretful.

Something silver flashes by my eyes.

Red spills from Adam's throat. His eyes stare at me, shocked, before turning glassy. He slumps to the floor. His pistol falls to the ground. I let out a shocked scream before Elijah covers my mouth with his hand. "Shhhh," he says against my ear. "There are still men here."

"What just happened?" I mouth the words, soundless against Elijah's palm.

"Peter kept a knife in his boot. I threw it at Adam's throat."

A whimper escapes me.

"Come on. Let's get out of here before someone comes looking." He picks up Adam's pistol and does something with the chamber. "Hell," he says. "Damn. Fuck."

"What's wrong?"

He tosses the pistol onto Adam's slumped body. "It was empty."

"All this time?"

"We'll do this the old-fashioned way." He leans down and grasps the knife. When he pulls, Adam's eyes open slightly. He looks confused, like he doesn't remember the past few minutes. Elijah grasps the knife differently, and I realize he plans to finish Adam off.

"Wait."

Elijah looks back, incredulous. "He was going to torture you."

"He also saved me from Peter."

"Which wouldn't have happened if he didn't kidnap you."

I know that Adam Bisset is not a good man. He should be taken to prison—a real prison, not one in the basement of a church. But killing a defenseless man doesn't feel right. The shock of realizing the gun was empty the whole time makes me uneasy. He isn't hurting us right now. This isn't self-defense. This would be murder. "No," I whisper.

"Holly." Elijah's voice is rough. "This bastard is the reason I touched you. The reason I... violated you. He should die for what he did to you."

"What he did to us," I say, my hand on Elijah's arm. "He violated you, too."

A dark laugh. "He wasn't so wrong. It was a good time for me."

I'm not sure about that. No one wants to be forced. Even knowing Adam's sins, I can't stand here and witness him be killed. "Let's just leave him."

Elijah wants to argue. He almost does. His mouth opens. And closes.

Then he turns and leads me away. I glance into Adam's dark eyes. There's gratitude. That's the last bit of shadow I see before Elijah leads me into the blinding light.

CHAPTER FIFTEEN
HOLLY

H E LEADS ME through a different way than before, a more circuitous route that lets us out directly into a dark copse of trees. Without a word he begins to push through the foliage, and I follow him with silent determination, ignoring the sting of branches and the pull of leaves.

It's day when we emerge from the church.

Day turns into night.

The sun bleeds over the horizon in red-purple rays by the time we stop for a break. The forest has changed in the hours that passed. It's become less damp, more sparse. There are no buildings in sight. He points to a flat rock, where I gratefully collapse. The coming sun casts only enough light to be eerie, without illuminating more than a few feet ahead of us.

"We'll rest for a few minutes," he says. "I want to find some shelter before the heat of midday."

My lips are already parched. How long will I last in the elements without food or water?

In the bright dawning sun it's clear he's strong. Broad shoulders. Muscled legs. He's wearing only jeans and a torn gray T-shirt. The bruises that cover his arms don't detract from his ability. Tendrils of red light illuminate a network of cuts.

They only show that he can survive anything. Everything.

"No," I say softly.

He turns back to me, green eyes flashing dangerously. "No?"

This is the first time I've been able to really see him. I've spent hours in a locked cell with him, but like the church, he was shrouded from view.

Now I see that he's commanding and strong. That much I expected from the way he spoke.

The part where he's handsome, I didn't see that coming. He could be on the set of some superhero movie, his face smudged with dirt, several days' growth darkening his jaw, walking away from an explosion. His eyes are striking green and gold, his hair a dark brown.

The boy was cute. This man is the grown up version, rugged and dark.

A man this dangerous shouldn't also be beautiful.

"I want some answers before I go anywhere with you."

"You were happy enough to leave the goddamn church without answers."

"Tell me about the guns."

He freezes for only half a second. It's a small thing, that reaction, but I'm watching for it, and I saw it. "You let me think you were stealing something, like jewels."

"You made the assumption. I didn't correct you."

"So it's true. You stopped stealing diamonds and started stealing guns. God."

"What does it matter? I'm not stealing anything right now."

"Of course it matters! I write children's books, for God's sake. And you're saying that you—what? That you're some kind of entrepreneurial warlord? That you buy and sell weapons?"

"Entrepreneurial warlord has a nice ring to it."

"This isn't funny."

"I'm not laughing. But we need to move before they follow our trail."

I stand and face him, knowing I'm dirty, a complete mess. Hungry. Thirsty. I'm weak in every way but one—stubbornness. "I'm not going anywhere with you."

"You are if I have to carry you, Holland Frank."

That's the only warning he gives me before bending down. His shoulder jams my stomach, and I cough at the sudden pressure. Then I'm hoisted over his shoulder in a fireman's carry.

"Let me down." I beat at his shoulders with my fists. It's like boxing a mountain. He doesn't even register the blows. He just keeps walking. "Asshole. Bastard. Thief."

He stops suddenly, and the momentum rolls me off his body. He pushes me against a tree, and I realize it was a careful maneuver. Everything he does is a careful maneuver. God, even ending up in the goddamn prison cell was probably done with grace. His face is inches from mine, and finally, finally I can see the beautiful gold lines in his green eyes. "I am an asshole. I am a bastard, and I'll own up to that. But I'm not a thief. I never was."

"The diamond."

"It was returned." He studies my eyes. "But then, you already knew that."

I look away, slightly to the right—the same way the Mona Lisa does, not really meeting his eyes. "So what? It made the news. And why shouldn't I know what happened? You made me an accomplice when you put that diamond in my backpack."

He gives me a crooked smile. "An accomplice? Is that what you think?"

"Of course it's what I think. God."

"And did you see that the men responsible were caught?"

"They were tried and convicted. They served jail time. Unlike you."

"You were glad I wasn't caught, weren't you?"

"Of course not. I should have called the FBI. Or Interpol. Or whoever."

He nuzzles my cheek. "You were glad. Admit it."

God. I was relieved. And frustrated with myself. And I still had that itchy, achy feeling that I didn't fully understand until years later. Sometimes I'm still not sure I fully understand. No one has affected me like him. "I'm not admitting anything."

He breathes in deep against my neck, and I'm transported back eight years. I can smell the yellow honeysuckle in the fence, hear the bells tolling in the cathedral. "I missed you, Holly."

"You didn't even know me."

"With your vicious fucking mermaids."

There's no reason to laugh—none. No reason that I should find that hilarious. It must be the total lack of food and water. It must be light deprivation making me insane. I push at his shoulder, but it's completely ineffectual. "They're only vicious because the dragons are so... they're so..."

"Terrible," he says, his voice severe. "I know."

My smile fades. "Go to hell, Elijah, or whoever you are."

"Elijah Michael North. Sergeant First Class. 452-48-9472."

"That sounds like name, rank, and serial number."

"Because that's what it is."

"You share that if you've been captured."

He leans down to bite the place where my shoulder meets my neck. I can't help but arch into him, and the zing of pain makes me moan. What a messed-up situation. What a terrible time to find someone hot. "Consider me captured," he murmurs.

"You're telling me that you joined the army?"

"I'm telling you that I joined the army, yes. Before we met."

I push him away, for real this time, and he

finally moves. The clearing doesn't give me nearly enough room to pace. I rub my hands on my arms, but the dawn is still too cold. Or maybe the cold is coming from inside. "And the diamond?"

"My mission. I was pulled into a special counterterrorism task force. The person who wanted the diamond, the person who financed the theft, had ties to a cell in Paris. I had to steal the diamond and make it believable in order to gain access to him."

I blink at him. "What's a terrorist doing in France?"

"They're everywhere, sweetheart. At least they were eight years ago."

"That's what you're doing now? Tracking terrorists? Tricking them into thinking you're one of them? Finding out their secrets so you can put them behind bars?"

"Yes."

"I don't believe you. God, you're as bad as Adam. Lying about being part of Interpol."

"He's not lying about that. As to where his true loyalties lie, that's still a question. I'm not even sure he knows the answer to that."

I feel torn between two men, pulled apart at the seams. It's like they're tugging and tugging with every lie, with every attempt to make me trust them. And in the end, I'm the one who unravels. "You know what? Fine. He's an Interpol agent. You're a soldier. Have a nice life."

With that I turn and stomp away from him. I've only taken three steps when a weight slams me onto the grassy forest floor. The breath whooshes out of me, and I cough my indignation into the dirt. He's gentle as he turns me over, righting my clothes and tucking a wild piece of hair behind my ear. "You're not going anywhere," he says, sounding almost regretful. Almost, but not quite.

"Why do you care where I go? I'm not holding your diamond in my backpack?"

He's leaning over me, his powerful arms flexing in the bloodred light. "Did you think I gave a fuck about that? I could have taken it from you at the crepes place if I really wanted to. I could have sent men into your goddamn hotel room. I kept coming back to you because I couldn't stay away."

"You stayed away from me just fine for eight years," I retort.

That crooked smile again. It's lethal. "Which one makes you angry? That I used you to hold the diamond? Or that I left you once I did?"

"Both," I say, snarling the word. I feel like one of those vicious mermaids he mentioned. And he's a dragon, holding me down with his talons, keeping me away from water.

"I'm not staying away now," he says, nudging me between my legs. Somehow he's settled himself there. As if he belongs. As if he's come home.

I buck my hips, but it doesn't dislodge him. "I hate you."

"No one gets me hot, Holly. Just kissing you was better than the sex I've had since then."

My eyes close in bitter defeat. Tears leak out of my eyes and stream down my cheeks. It's what I wanted then, what I've wanted for so long, and I hate that. "Do it, then."

"You're going to ask nicely."

It makes me want to hurt him, even as I surrender. I reach up as if I'm going to kiss him, and he bends down to meet me. And I do kiss him. Once. Softly. Before biting down on his bottom lip. He grunts in pain, and I taste blood. His hips roll against me. It's made him harder.

"Ah, sweetheart," he says on a rough laugh. "You're going to beg before this is over."

CHAPTER SIXTEEN

ELIJAH

EIGHT YEARS AGO, I walked away from the most beautiful girl in the world.

I don't bother telling her that because she wouldn't believe me. And anyways, it's not precisely a compliment. I walked away knowing that other men would kiss her and fuck her.

Damned if I'm going to do it again.

I saw you. I wanted you. And I take what I want. It doesn't have to be more complicated than that, Holly. I said those words to her once, but they were just a fantasy then.

"You need to understand something. The US government doesn't give a fuck what happens to you. And Adam? He wants you gone now that you've seen his face and learned his secret. I'm the only thing standing between you and death right now."

Her eyes are a storm. And she wonders why I picked her up at the Louvre. She wonders if she's as pretty as her sister, if she's special. There's a universe inside her. When I bite her, it's because I can taste the wildness, the saltwater rain.

She's crying now. Her hips move in a primal rhythm against mine. It's too much, an overload of emotion after being held in captivity, after escaping. I should give her space to recover. Instead I'm going to fuck her like I should have done eight years ago. I've given enough of my life to upholding the rules. I'm taking her even with broken bones and a black eye. With cigar burns on my chest. All of it makes my dick harder, because she's my proof of life. Proof that I made it out of that hellhole. Proof that I'm still alive.

She tears at my clothes, her hands fumbling and clumsy. I have to push her away to undress myself. When I'm naked, she makes a sound of pain and touches one of the whip marks. Fuck him. I take her fingers and grind them into the red welt until I grunt in pain. She yanks her hand back. "Stop it," she says, crying harder.

This is how I want her. Not laid out in some hotel bed with a sultry smile. Not wearing pantyhose and a red dress. Oh hell, I want her that way too. But now, right now I want her as raw as possible. Only her body covered in dirt and sweat and grass. I pull her clothes away to reveal pink nipples and a flush that spreads across her breasts.

I suck the tight buds into my mouth, and it's heaven. If those burns and broken bones were the price of tasting her, they were worth it. It's a sick and twisted thought. In a perfect world the horror that I see on a daily basis would never touch her. But it did touch her. Adam kidnapped her. Somehow, in a world full of men and women, he found her for me.

Her skin tastes of sweat, and it's perfect. This is how animals fuck. I move to her other breast and bite down on the plump, smooth, pale skin, leaving teeth marks. She lets out a little shriek, and I bite harder. Only when she subsides, when she submits, do I release her.

"Beg," I mutter.

She shakes her head on the grass.

I take one of her wrists and flatten it to the ground. Then the other. Her hands are beside her head, exactly like they were all those years ago. Except then we were younger and more innocent and fully clothed. I was bound by basic human decency. All of that's gone now. I'm straddling her stomach naked, my heavy cock resting between her tits.

"Beg or I won't fuck you, and you'll never

know. Always wonder."

Her fists clench. "I hate you."

"You don't have to stop hating me. You just have to say please."

Her tits bounce so pretty as she tries to buck me off. She's burning up for this. The flush is all over her body, red and warm. "Please," she whimpers. And then louder. "Please."

"Fuck yes." I pull back between her legs and use my palm to spread her wide. She's already swollen and wet and ready for me. "How many men you let inside, sweetheart?"

"That's none of your business." Prim. She's fucking prim, and it's hot.

"One? Two?"

"Two, if you have to know."

"They ever slap you?"

Her eyes go wide. "What?"

I place a well-aimed slap to her pretty cunt, and she jolts. "No!"

"No, they didn't slap your pussy? Or no, don't do it again?"

"I don't know," she moans.

She may not know, but I do. This pussy needs to be slapped well and often. I place another slap right against her slit, my fingers coming away wet. Another one, this time aimed right at her clit, and she almost has an orgasm. So I help her hold it at bay by slapping the inside of her thigh. Then the other one. She sucks in a breath at the sharp pain.

Only when she's braced for another slap do I finally notch my cock against her pussy.

"I've waited long enough for you. Eight years of wondering what your pussy felt like. Eight years of regret. I did the right thing once but not again. You're mine now."

She's drenched and throbbing. Physically burning from the slaps, and it encloses my cock in a tight, wet slide. I shove myself into her in one hard thrust, and she cries harder.

I don't pause. She doesn't want that from me, and I don't want to give it. Instead I grasp her hips to hold her steady and pound into her with every ounce of strength left. Starvation and beatings. My heart could stop at any fucking second, and this is the way I'd want to go. Something drops down between her tits. Sweat? Tears? Maybe both. I probably needed recovery time, too, but I'm not going to get it. Not when she's moaning and bucking and clenching on my cock, goddamn, and then she's coming. I let myself spill over in a glorious, painful, blinding climax.

The aftershocks ripple tight around my dick,

and I yank myself out. It's like leaving a plug. I go from burning electricity to the cold morning air on my cock. I tumble myself to the grass—so I don't smother her. That's the excuse I use in my head. The truth is I'm not ready to cuddle and have an after-sex chat. The only feelings inside me are feral. I want to drag her by the hair to the nearest cave and fuck her again—raw and hard, until her cunt's overflowing with my seed.

This is what happens when you torture a man, when you keep him in the dark for days, for weeks. I'm stripped down to my basest nature.

CHAPTER SEVENTEEN

HOLLY

I LIE ON the grass, sweat cooling on my body, both mine and his. My cheeks heat, my body still imprinted with the feel of his. How many men you let inside, sweetheart? There had been two of them, but they had never touched me like Elijah.

"Do you think they're behind us?"

"We've walked a good six miles, and I've been covering our tracks. So, no. I don't think they're about to burst through the trees, if that's what you mean. On the other hand, I wouldn't linger. We have a long way to go before we can stop."

"Adam might not have made it." I can't believe I'm hoping someone died. I should be hoping he survived, but I'm so tired. The kind of tired that feels like physical pain.

"Maybe. Maybe not. He wasn't the only man there, though."

I can't help the whimper that escapes. "I'm

not sure I have much more left."

"You'll walk. You'll walk because you have to."

My eyes close in exhaustion. It's embarrassing to feel weak in front of this man. Even with more days of captivity he's clearly stronger than me. Stronger than most men, probably. A warrior, like the kind who fought with a sword and shield in ancient Greece.

"We have a few minutes," he says gruffly. "Tell me about your next book."

"What next book?" I ask automatically, though I'm stalling for time. Of course I have a next book. The question is only whether I'll tell him about it. Sex is intimate, but telling him about my unwritten book is letting him even deeper into my mind.

"More tooth fairies? Or are they teeth fairies in plural?"

My lips curve in a reluctant smile. He's trying to distract me. My feet scream in pain, my side aches. Every muscle shakes even as I'm lying on the ground. I'm a wreck of a human, but when he cracks a stupid joke, it doesn't seem so horrible.

"It's not about a tooth fairy."

"What, then? Mermaids? Dragons?"

"Not a fantasy creature. This book is about a

human woman."

"Human women are my fantasy."

I ignore this. "She's been dropped into a strange world where everything is upside down and colorful. It's terrifying, but it also makes her feel alive. Like an *Alice in Wonderland* except more violent."

"More violent? I thought she chops off heads in the original."

"That's the Queen of Hearts. But in my version, it's Alice who's violent. She's like a kickass heroine in a blue pinafore and a leg strap for her dagger."

"That's one of the hottest things I've ever heard."

"Anyway, it's not actually Wonderland, where she ends up. There's no white rabbit or Cheshire cat. They're only figments of her imagination, because she's actually walking through the dark parts of her own mind. She's locked in an asylum, you see. She's insane."

He sits up, rubbing a hand over his jaw. "Is that what's happening to you?"

"I don't know." My eyes squeeze shut. "What if I'm still in that prison cell? What if the plane crashed on some tropical island and this is all some fever-induced dream? What if I'm actually locked in a padded cell, and I only imagined you?"

"You really are a goddamn delight," he says softly, echoing the same compliment he gave me eight years ago in a hole-in-the-wall restaurant. I'd had a priceless diamond in my backpack at the time, only I hadn't known it then. He'd known it, though. And he'd let me walk away with it. It was a huge freaking risk, even if he was pretty sure he'd see me again for our date.

"So how do you go from being a soldier to this... this..."

"I'm still a soldier. Only I fight a different way." He sighs. "As to how I got started, I can thank the wonders of psychological testing for that. Most men are put into basic combat. Sometimes they're pulled out for specific programs, like computers or medicine. Me? I suppose they saw something in my results that said I'd be great at lying. And the hell of it is, they're right."

"It's tearing you apart, isn't it?"

"Why would you think that? I'm great at my job. The best."

"Maybe it's not me who's wearing a blue pinafore and a leg strap for my dagger. Maybe it's you. You go around being violent, slashing at everything you can see, but in reality you're lost."

His expression turns cold. His eyes could freeze me. "Don't try to psychoanalyze me. Trust me, that's above our pay grade."

"It doesn't take a psychiatrist to know you're messed up about your parents."

"Don't."

Why am I being so hard on him? I don't go around psychoanalyzing people I meet, but this is different. We were locked up together. We escaped together. And now we've had sex. There's a primal connection between us. Certainty roots inside me. Certainty that this man needs me to dig around in his emotional wounds. He's got them clenched so tight in his fists that they'll never really heal this way. "Or maybe you're the one in a padded room. Maybe they locked you up after you killed your father, and everything else, meeting me, being a soldier, stealing the diamond, that was all a medically aided dream."

He growls at me. "You have no idea what you're talking about."

"No? Then tell me the truth."

"I wish that were the case," he bursts out. "I wish someone would lock me up for what I did. Not for killing my father. For failing to protect my mother. For being too damn late to protect her. Doesn't matter that I was too young—that's why I belonged in that cell. Or a padded white room. Wherever the hell they put people like me, people no one can trust."

"I trust you," I whisper.

He stands and stares at me, his eyes cold. I know what he's going to say before the echo of the past emerges from his lips. "You should know better than to talk to someone like me. You should be afraid of me. And most of all, you shouldn't trust me."

CHAPTER EIGHTEEN

ELIJAH

I WASN'T EXAGGERATING when I said the United States government doesn't care what happens to a civilian during a deep-cover operation.

They know I have to do horrible things to survive. Adam could have fucked her, hurt her, killed her, and I could have done nothing to jeopardize my mission.

Not even save her life.

I'm supposed to be waiting in that jail cell right now, ready to die for my country, close by in case I can actually stop a terrorist attack. I could have escaped the first day. I could have left any goddamn time, but my cover meant staying there.

My orders were to remain with the operation.

Instead I'm babysitting a woman in the forests of northern France.

I don't want to see the look on the lieutenant colonel's face when he finds out I fucking deserted. Because that's exactly how he'll look at it. The fact that Holly is an innocent caught in the crossfire won't matter to him.

The whisper of water cuts through the regular forest sounds, and I switch directions. It's west when we need to be going south, the terrain more rugged this way, but it's worth it. My mouth is parched, and Holly looks like she's about to fall over. Sure enough, the soil becomes more soft and loamy. Soon the babble becomes a brook, and my throat clenches in anticipation.

She drops to her knees in the muddy edge, pressing her face into the water. It's animalistic and strangely sexy, seeing her drink that way. Then she's looking up at me, her lips glistening, water dripping down her chin. It's a purely sensual look, though she probably has no idea. "Aren't you going to drink?" she asks.

A man's body is stupid enough to get hard, even when I clearly need the strength for other things. I drop down beside her, letting the mud soak the denim of my jeans and press my face into the water. I drink like a wolf, opening my mouth and letting it fill the space. A hard swallow. Beside me she's cupping water and gulping it. I take her wrist, and water spills down her arms. "Slow down," I say, my voice gruff. "You'll throw up."

She stares at me, and for a second I think she's going to cry. Or maybe vomit. Or maybe ignore me and keep drinking. Instead she says in a droll tone, "Worst date ever."

A strange joy sings through my chest, that she can find humor in this moment. I've eaten sweet blueberry crepes and delicately cooked quail with this woman, but none of them can touch the delicious moment of cool water.

I have to force myself to stop before I've had my fill, too.

Then I rip off my shirt and wring it out in the water. I dab the corner onto her cheek where there's dried blood. That must have happened when she escaped. When Peter attacked her. I should have killed him sooner. I left him bleeding out in the church. He's gone now.

Too late.

Every time I love someone, I'm too fucking late.

Love. No. I can't love her. I can't love her because it will only make her die. It's the logic that comes from a child who saw his mother's life drain from her eyes. It doesn't matter that I'm grown-up now. It still holds an important, unshakeable truth.

I carefully pull her shirt over her arms, exposing her breasts in dirt-stained lace. She's beautiful. Sensual. Devastating. But right now I'm focused on the wound at her side. I touch the edges, which are blue and yellow from the bleeding inside.

It's one thing to know she must be injured. Another thing to see it in the light.

My hands are shaking. "I'm sorry," I say, my voice uneven.

"It's fine." She gives me a brave, tremulous smile. "It didn't hurt."

For a second I stare at her, knowing she's lying. Then I realize she means back in the clearing, when I fucked her. She thinks I'm apologizing for being careless with her injuries. And it's so kind, the way she wants to forgive me for fucking her raw.

Even though she doesn't know what I've done.

Suddenly I want her to know. I want her to see what a monster I am, so she stops looking up at me with those eyes full of hope and humor and light.

I'm not a man who deserves forgiveness.

"I could have walked out of that cell at any time."

She blinks, not quite believing. Not wanting

to believe. "What?"

"Every time they came in to beat me, I could have escaped. Every time Peter took a cigar to my skin, I could have broken his neck. I didn't have a key to that lock, but I didn't need one. The key was in my hands."

Confusion tightens her brow. "Why are you telling me this?"

"So you understand." I trace the angry red line where the metal bar cut into her flesh. It hurt her so badly, and even now it might kill her. Infection in a goddamn forest with no access to medicine or even soap. "I did this to you. I pushed you through the bars."

"So I could escape," she says, but she sounds less certain now.

"I almost broke you in half, but not so you could escape. I did it so that I could stay there. So that I could stay there without blowing my cover."

She shakes her head. "Why did you need to stay? Why did you—"

"My cover? That took eighteen months to establish. Eighteen months of pretending to be a lowlife, of doing horrible things so they'd trust me. Eighteen months of my life." I snap my fingers, knowing I'm being an asshole. "Gone.

Down the drain."

"Why are you angry at me?"

Why am I angry at her? I'm not sure whether I'm mad at her or myself, but I'm goddamn furious. "Because you were going to get raped, understand? Whether it happened that day or later, Peter was going to hurt you. Adam was going to fuck you. And I shouldn't have cared about that. I'm well trained not to care about that, but I couldn't let it happen."

I'm pleading by the end of it, and her eyes aren't furious with me. She looks soft and understanding. She looks like everything I want, and nothing that I deserve.

"You saved me," she says simply.

I shake my head. "No, goddamn you. I hurt you."

"You saved me," she says again, pushing down her leggings, showing her sweet, pink pussy. My body doesn't know that I'm full of guilt and regret and rage. It has the predictable response to seeing her pretty body exposed. I'm hard as a log in a matter of seconds.

She puts her hands on my chest and pushes— not hard enough to knock over anything, but there I go, toppling into the shallow water, letting her climb me. She fights with the wet denim to release my cock, and then she's holding me with those clever fingers.

I drop my head back and look up at the blinding sun.

Heaven. How did I ever find myself here?

I belong in the other place. I belong back in that cell. It was my job and my mission, but more than that, it was the only thing I deserved. Now I have her gentle hands working me, too soft, too soft. A more terrible torture than Peter's whip, her too-soft hands.

Then she climbs over my lap. She's adorably awkward, the way she angles my cock toward her pussy. It's like she's hardly ever done this. We fit perfectly, I know that from last time, I know that from my dreams, but it takes her long minutes, hours, days to wedge me inside her. It takes an eternity of pressure as her body surrounds my cock.

Wet heat grips me all the way down, and I shout toward the sky.

"You saved me," she says, bearing down, pressing until her pussy lips touch the thatch of hair at the base of my cock, pulling me with little pulses of her inner muscles. "Say it."

"Never." I'm holding myself with both my elbows in the mud. I'm completely open to her.

She sets the pace. She decides when to raise her body and when to twist back down.

"Admit it, Elijah. Whoever you are."

I grit my teeth against the sheer pleasure. "Mermaid. Siren. Fairy."

She gives a small laugh that turns into a moan. "You saved—"

With a hard upward thrust I cut off the last word. "No."

I flip us over so I can fuck her into the water, fuck her into the mud, fuck her into submission. "Do you want me to compromise everything I am? Do you want me to give up everything I have? It's already yours, Holly. I'm yours to command."

I slam my mouth down on hers. My hands drag up and down the length of her body, heedless of the mud and her injuries, feeling her in her raw state.

She moans as I tilt my hips to find that spot inside her. "Yes. Yes. Yes."

CHAPTER NINETEEN
HOLLY

I THOUGHT I knew what tiredness felt like. Thirty-six hours of flights with no sleep. A hike in the Grand Canyon. A particularly evil spin class at my local gym. I've known exhaustion, but nothing has ever come close to this. My entire body throbs. There's an invisible knife stabbing my head. My heart seems to thump at double its normal rate. Every step sends nails into the soles of my feet.

The world goes dark.

I wake up on the ground, with my face wet. Elijah is holding me, shaking me gently, using his shirt to wipe something red from my cheek. "There you are," he says, and though his voice sounds calm, almost dry, I sense the urgency underneath.

The sun beats down on me, relentless. "Can't."

Something soft brushes my forehead. Maybe a

kiss. "We need to move, sweetheart."

I force my eyes open. "Go without me. Please."

Green eyes flash with anger—and maybe fear. "Absolutely not."

"Come back," I mumble, hoping he'll understand what I mean. He can leave me here in the sun and get help. That's the only way I see out of this. My feet won't take another step. My body won't move another inch. My mind feels full of damp cotton.

A strong arm shoves underneath me. Then I'm lifted into the air, held suspended against his hard chest. My arms move automatically to wrap around his neck.

"No," I whisper.

"Don't complain, sweetheart." His lips murmur against my ear. "I'm not leaving you behind. Ask me to do anything, anything else. I'd lie down and die with you before I'd walk away."

Tears squeeze from my eyes and slide down my cheeks. "Please."

I don't want him to die. That might happen if he carries me. He could survive on his own. Can he carry another human's weight? I'm only going to slow him down. There's no answer to my plea. He's implacable about this. It's not up for discussion.

There is no help I can offer him—so I give him the only form of strength I have left. My stories. My words. "Wonderland," I say, the word faintly slurred. "Do you want to hear more?"

"Yes," he says, his arms secure beneath me. "Tell me your story."

There's no story, not really. Nothing already written or formed in my mind. When I'm half-dead from exhaustion isn't really the time to be my most creative, but here we are. "She goes in strong, using her knife and her cunning to defeat the creatures she meets, but then..."

"But then," he prompts when I fall silent.

"But then she hears about the evil queen, the Queen of Hearts. Everyone talks about her, everyone is afraid of her, and Alice thinks..." Tears stream harder. "She thinks she can run away, but she can't. She can't run anymore."

"Hell." He rubs the scruff of his jaw across my forehead, a scrape that jolts me back to awareness. "You don't have to tell this story."

"She runs and runs anyway, until there's nothing left. And then the Queen of Hearts finds her. The queen knows she's weak, and she chooses that moment to strike."

"No one's going to strike you. Not ever

again."

Consciousness hovers in front of me. It's like I'm deep underwater, and I can't find my way out. The words sound like they're far away, but they're spoken in my voice. "She can't fight back, because it's her sister. Her sister is the Queen of Hearts."

A gruff voice quiets me. "Easy. Easy now."

I'm not sure how much time passes. An hour. Two. Three. We stop again, and Elijah lays me down in a field while he picks figs and wild cress for us to eat. Then he lifts me again, and I close my eyes, gently jostled by the motion of walking, drifting in and out of sleep.

The nightmare comes for me again, even in broad daylight, brazen now.

The monster gnaws at my side, and I struggle to get away, but my arms won't move, I'm trapped in his jaws as he chews and chews. A man stands to the side, holding the leash of the monster. "Why do men usually take beautiful women?" he asks.

Something brings me back to alertness.

"Thank God," the same man says.

We're walking through a field, the stalks of something gold high enough to brush my feet as we pass. There's a small house up ahead. The front door opens, and a man steps onto the dirt. He's holding a shotgun. "Qui es-tu il demande?" he asks.

"My wife," Elijah says. "*Ma femme*. She's sick. Help."

The man does not look convinced. He holds the shotgun like a man well versed in shooting it. Weather and years have drawn deep lines into his face.

Then Elijah says, his voice more succinct, "L'aube arrive plus tôt chaque jour."

My drowsy mind struggles to interpret something about the dawn and its early arrival each day. Why is he telling that to a stranger?

A woman steps out. She slaps her hand on the man's arm, clearly unimpressed with his hold on the shotgun, and says something rapid-fire in French. "La nuit tombe plus tard chaque jour."

My tired mind struggles to make sense of the words with my rudimentary travel-dictionary French. The night arrives later each day. But her gesture is unmistakable.

Come in, the wave of her arm says, *you're safe here. You can rest.*

Relief is enough to send a fresh wave of tears down my cheeks. We're ushered into a modest home with an old flower-patterned couch. I'm laid there while the woman fetches tea. The hot liquid slides down my throat like a life force, replenishing me. Elijah spins a story about how we were picked up at the airport by an Uber that ended up being a fake, and taken at gunpoint to the country, where we were left behind, all of our luggage and money stolen.

The man offers to call the cops for us. La police.

My stomach clenches. There's no reason the police can't help. Adam kidnapped me. Of course we should file a report. Except some instinct warns me that it's dangerous.

"No," Elijah says. "They're long gone by now, and I'm sure their license was fake. We'll never get our things back, but my brother can help."

An old cell phone appears, battered, with the screen cracked. We all remain in the small room that appears to serve as the dining room, living room, and kitchen.

He dials a number by heart. "Hello? It's Elijah. Yeah, we ran into some trouble on our honeymoon. Holly's a little banged up. We both need some new identification."

"My sister," I whisper.

Elijah glances at me, then continues speaking. "Also, can you check in with Holly's sister? Yeah,

London must be worried sick. Remember, her maiden name's Frank."

I meet his green, green eyes. "Thank you," I say, eyes welling with tears again. I've become a watering pot. Exhaustion has brought every emotion to the surface. Fear, grief, worry, along with relief, elation, and a very unfortunate growing affection for the man beside me. I care about him more than I should. I understood what he really meant at the lake...

He did save me, but he didn't want to.

He does care about me, but he doesn't want to.

He may help me, but he's making no promises.

"We found some people who are helping us," he says, continuing to speak to his brother. "Let me hand the phone over and you can get the address."

The man speaks a mixture of French and broken English on the phone.

The words nuit and jour float around in my head. Night and day. A code, my mind whispers. It's as if they were exchanging a code.

It occurs to me that Elijah spoke a beautiful, fluent form of French when we were in the church. Now, in front of the couple, it's choppy and Americanized. That must be part of our disguise as honeymooners. Every part of him is calculated. That's what he means by deep cover. I wonder how much of him is truth. Maybe he doesn't even know the answer.

I whisper to him when the woman bustles at the stove, making something with bread and cheese for us. "Why didn't you call your lieutenant colonel?"

"I made my choice," he murmurs back. "And I chose you."

CHAPTER TWENTY

ELIJAH

I'VE MADE THE wrong choice.

Every part of my upbringing, every second of my training. Every cell in my body is certain that I should have hardened my heart to Holly Frank. Let her be raped or beaten. Or killed. It wouldn't be my fault. I wasn't the one who kidnapped her. I should have finished my mission.

Even calling my brother was a shot in the dark. We aren't what you'd call a close family. They took care of me as much as they could when they were home, stealing food when the pantry was empty, finding blankets when the gas turned off. But they were enlisted as soon as they could and never came back. They weren't there the final two years with our father.

They weren't there when I finally killed him and got justice for our mother.

Wrong, wrong, wrong. It's wrong that I'm

taking the hospitality of these nice people and pretending that Holly's my wife, but in these stolen moments it feels right.

The woman shows us upstairs to a small room with a quilted bedspread and an ancient, scarred dresser. The master bedroom, I understand. This is where the farmer and his wife sleep.

Some long-dormant manners remind me to object. We shouldn't displace them. The sofa will be fine. Or even the barn with a pile of straw. Hell, in my job sleeping in the field is a luxury sometimes. But then I look down at Holly's face, her delicate nose with its smattering of freckles, her full lips with their tempting peach color, and I know she needs this bed. I've seen men die on marches like the one she was just forced to endure.

The heart stops.

It's a miracle she lived. A miracle I never deserved. So I lay her down on the bedspread, where she closes her eyes, immediately asleep. Then I climb in beside her, gather her still body close as if I can ward away death, and sink deeply into dreams.

There are vicious mermaids and dragons in my sleep.

And a war that both sides are destined to lose.

✦   ✦   ✦

WHEN I WAKE, deep night has settled over the house. I glance out the scalloped pink curtains to the moon. It illuminates a wide, empty field. It's unlikely Adam could track us this far, but possible. Which damns me for taking these people's hospitality.

There's a bathroom adjacent to this room, with black-and-white tile and a claw-foot tub. I start the faucet and fill it halfway with steaming water. Then I return to Holly, who's still deeply asleep. I pull her clothes off gently, careful with the wound at her side, wincing at the bloody mass of her feet. Her body feels impossibly slight in my arms, far too small for a whole, healthy person.

I place her in the water, and she startles awake, gasping.

"Easy," I tell her. "I'm right here. I've got you." Her frightened eyes meet mine, and my heart wrenches. What the hell am I doing to her? How will I survive her?

"Elijah," she whispers before closing her eyes again.

So much trust.

I use a lavender-scented soap to wash the dirt and blood from her body. The water becomes a pale brown. I wash her feet tenderly, wincing at the cuts across the bottom. Then I go to work on her hair. The shampoo becomes a dull gray lather in her honey-toned hair. She probably needs an hour-long soak in a fresh tub of water to be fully clean, but her eyes flutter and her breath rises and falls—and it's enough for her to be alive right now.

My thumb brushes over her bottom lip, and her eyes open.

"Your brother?" she asks.

"He's on his way." At least I hope so.

It's possible he hung up the phone and then went back to work. We didn't have family reunions. We don't exchange Christmas cards. I have no idea what a real family would be like.

A few years ago when Liam left the military, he started his own private security firm. The only reason I know that is because I got a letter from a lawyer in the mail giving me a one-third share in the business.

Pretty fucking trusting considering I could be a psycho like our father.

I accepted the shares, technically, signing the paperwork and sending it back via the lawyers, but I've never participated in any other way. A ridiculous amount of money gets deposited into a bank account in my name every quarter.

This is the first time I've called the number on the paperwork.

"You trust him more than the police?" she asks.

The last time we spoke, I was an angry fourteen-year-old with a bad attitude. Liam had enlisted with a gruff goodbye and left without looking back. Was I pissed at him? No. I was jealous. Then a couple years later Josh left, too.

That's when shit really got bad at home.

And now here we are, years later. It's Elijah, I said to him. Yeah, we ran into some trouble on our honeymoon. Holly's a little banged up. We both need some new identification.

He might have said, who the hell is this?

He might have said, fuck no.

Instead he said, "On it." It was like we'd been working together for years. I knew in those two words that he'd move heaven and earth to accomplish the mission.

"Yeah," I say, my voice rough.

"The couple? What was it you said to them about the night and the dawn?"

Of course she noticed that. "It's a code."

"What does it mean?"

"That we're in trouble. That we need help. That we mean no harm."

Actually it means that we're part of the resistance fighting the French government. I took a chance that the farmers would know such a code and respect it, the same way they respect the seasons and the storms and the old ways of life.

She's like deadweight in the bath, her head leaning back on the curved lip. She's like a doll I can move however I want, and fuck, I'm done restraining myself. Holly may not fully understand what she's gotten into with me, but before this night is over, she will.

I pick up one beautiful pale leg and drape it over the side of the tub. Then I lift the other and do the same. She's completely open to me, a pink flower.

"Here?" she asks, her voice lazy.

I slide my hand down her stomach and cup her pussy. "Everywhere."

Her sex accepts my fingers like they were made to hold me. I slide in and out, learning every square inch of her, pressing on that place that makes her breath catch.

She tenses, and I flick her clit with my thumb—a little too hard.

It's punishment. "Relax, sweetheart. Give in."

Her hips lift, and I think she's going to fight me.

I would enjoy subduing her but not right now, not when she's so weak. Her lids rise, revealing those dark pools of lust. It releases electricity through my body, and my cock flexes against the outside of the tub. I want to fuck her, fuck her, fuck her, but this isn't about me.

It's about her and the way she melts into the white ceramic. The way she becomes soft and malleable in my hands. The way it gets her wetter to give in.

I circle her clit with slow deliberation, making her wait and yearn. Enjoying the way she moans in the small space. "We're married now," I say, my voice low. "I can do anything I want with this sweet body. I can fuck you in the bathroom, in the kitchen. Wherever you are, I can press you against the wall and get inside my favorite place."

She moans again, and I know the words make her hot. She likes the idea of being taken by force, my little mermaid, my own personal siren. I crash against the rocks, not because she sings. I crash because she exists. Because I'm weak, and she's strong.

So I give her more words, more fantasies. If she were my wife, I would only let her out of bed for the pleasure of dragging her back. I would wrap my belt around her throat and make her beg to suck my cock. "I'm going to lie next to you on that bed, and whenever my dick wants a nice warm place to rest, I'm going to spread your legs. There'll be nothing you can do, no way to say no because you're already mine."

On the last word, the word mine, I flick her clit, and she comes with a high, keening cry, one that surely the couple downstairs will hear and recognize. It's the sound of ownership.

CHAPTER TWENTY-ONE
HOLLY

I'M LEARNING HOW to knead dough with Marisol when Elijah comes downstairs. He looks fresh in a worn button-down shirt and jeans. The farmer's clothes. I'm wearing a peasant blouse and a long skirt that make me look like I belong among the wheat stalks.

And my hands are covered in flour.

Elijah comes up to me from behind and grasps my waist, planting a kiss on my cheek. The move makes me blush, but I can't say anything because we're supposed to be married. Marisol gives me a secret smile, and I know she thinks it's because this is new. New as in we're having our honeymoon. Not new as in we've been pretending for the past twenty-four hours.

"Like this," Marisol says, doing something smooth and knowledgeable with her hands.

My copy looks much more clumsy.

Even though I've been copying her from the

beginning, my dough looks more lumpy and harder than hers. It's clear that I didn't miss my calling by becoming a fiction writer instead of a baker, but there's something soothing about working with the food in my hands. Elijah snakes his hands under my skirt, and I squirm away, spraying him with a little bit of excess flour.

"Don't," I say, laughing. "I'll be lucky if my dough rises."

"You're making something rise," he says.

It's easy to imagine this is how it would be if we were actually a newly married couple, if I were sore from having sex with my husband, if we were recovering from a dishonest Uber driver. The truth is much less optimistic. He's an undercover operative in some shadow military department, and I'm... me. Holly Frank. Best-selling author of children's novels. The scariest thing in my life is a speaking gig in front of sixth graders.

We were thrown together, literally, but we don't belong together.

You're mine, he told me in the bathroom, but that's only sex talk.

It's not real. The way he took me again and again last night, spreading me wide, holding down my wrists, or turning me onto my hands and knees, that was real.

That's the only thing we have.

There's a knock at the door, and Elijah moves quickly. In a blur he has a knife from the block and he's standing beside the door. Marisol lets out a little shriek of surprise and fear, and I block her with my body. Instinctively I understand that Adam might have found us here, and I don't want our hosts to be hurt for helping us.

Elijah uses the blade to move aside the white eyelet-pattern curtain. There's a pause where the entire room holds its breath. Then he relaxes. The change is infinitesimal but very real. If I were an animal, the hair raised on the back of my neck would slowly lower to normal.

He opens the door, and someone walks in. Someone who is very clearly his brother. If I were to have passed him on the street, I would know he's related to Elijah. The same tall build with broad shoulders and tanned skin. The same hard nose and firm mouth. Most of all they share the same vibrant green eyes.

Liam nods at Elijah.

Elijah nods back, his expression closed.

That's when I realize that these two men are virtually strangers. Elijah may have called his brother for help, but these are not men who regularly get together for Thanksgiving. My heart clenches as they both regard each other warily, two wolves wondering what the other will do.

"I'm so glad you're here," I say, breaking the silence. I throw my arms at Liam, and luckily for me, he catches me in a hug. "It was so awful. We didn't know who to call—and on our honeymoon! You're such a good big brother for coming."

He falls into the deception easily, tousling my hair as the quintessential sibling. "Not the most lucky start, but we're going to make sure you two have a good time. I promise."

"My sister. Did you talk to her? She must be so worried. I promised her I'd text."

"I reached out," he says, his nod casual, those green eyes solemn. They're a richer color, giving the impression of depth. Elijah's eyes are more hazel with gold lines. "Didn't quite catch her by phone before I got on the plane, but I'm sure I'll reach her soon."

Disappointment sinks in my stomach. It had been nice to imagine that London had hooked up with some stranger and turned off her ringer for a couple weeks. It's not even an entirely unlikely scenario. She could have come back to the world and found my messages about flying to France. She could be at the embassy waiting for me.

Wishful thinking.

Swallowing my worry, I step backward and gesture to Marisol. Her husband has come in behind her. "These are our hosts," I say to Liam. "They've been so kind since we lost everything."

He steps forward and offers a handshake. "You have my gratitude for taking care of my brother. Family means the world to me. If you ever need anything, I'll leave my number."

"Do we have to leave right away?" I ask. "We're making bread."

Liam glances at Elijah, who studies the conversation as if he's an outsider. There's something very alone about him, and my heart clenches. "There's time," Elijah says. "Maybe I can take a walk with my brother while you finish making lunch."

"Of course." I reach up to place a kiss on Elijah's cheek. "See you when you get back, honey."

It feels like a wifely thing to do, and it occurs to me that Liam North may think we're actually married. That's what Elijah had said over the phone.

He watches me with speculation in his eyes. And caution.

It's a good thing I have no intention of harming Elijah. I don't think his brother would allow that to happen. Strangers or not, there's a bond between these men. Something that drew him across the world based on a single phone call. I understand that bond because it's the same one I share with my sister. If she's in trouble, there's nothing I wouldn't do for her.

London, where are you?

We've covered for each other; we've supported each other.

We've been sisters in every sense of the word, despite our differences, but we've never had to search for each other. The world is too vast, and the risk of failure too great.

CHAPTER TWENTY-TWO

ELIJAH

I RAISE MY hand and let the tips of wheat stalks scrape across my palm. Even with a hundred bruises, even with broken bones, it feels fucking incredible to be alive. Or maybe I just feel so good because of the massive amount of sex I've just had.

"She seems nice," Liam says.

I give him a sideways glance. "We're not actually married."

He doesn't seem surprised. "She still seems nice."

Nice? I suppose. She seems fucking sexy. Maddening. Consuming. Those are the words that I think of about Holly Frank. I want to swallow down her light so I can keep it inside me. Nice? That's a foreign word compared to my feelings. "Appreciate you coming."

"Of course," he says, which is a lie. We owe each other nothing.

"Josh?" Our middle brother.

"Alive," he says, which about sums up the North brothers. We're survivors. "I'm glad you called, even if the circumstances are shit. You're favoring your left side. Broken ribs?"

"A couple."

He says nothing. "Don't suppose you want a doctor?"

"That's not a priority."

"I disagree about that, but I think I lost my right to be the protective big brother a long time ago. There are some fake passports, fresh credit cards. A private jet at the airport."

"Thank you."

"Is it the girl? Is she trouble?"

We're walking through the stalks where a tractor has come through, mowing them right down to the ground. I give him a hard look. "Like you said, you lost the right to be the protective big brother a long time ago."

"You want an apology?" he asks, his tone light.

"Fuck no."

"Because I don't mind giving you one. It's owed."

"There's nothing owed. I called you, and you came." That's more proof of familial responsibility than a thousand apologies would be. It means I'm indebted to him. The money in the account? That meant nothing. Helping me protect Holly is the only thing I need.

"Are you going to read me in?"

That's military speak for giving him the classified details. "I was on a mission. Holly was going to get hurt, and the only way to stop it was to go AWOL."

He whistles. "They're not going to like that."

Liam doesn't even know the lieutenant colonel. He was a different division altogether, but all commanding officers are alike in this regard. No one would be pleased with me. The life of one civilian woman does not compare to the mission. That may be a hard truth that the American people don't want to think about, but it's true. I understood the order of things until I realized that Holland Frank was the same girl from my past. By then it was too late.

"I'm here as long as you need me. Josh is on standby."

Hell. I'm not a man of many emotions, but a few of them flood my veins. I've been alone for so long, facing the world and fighting everyone in it. There was nothing to live for before Holly. Now I have a family waiting to help.

I stop walking and face my brother. "I'm worried about Adam Bisset. He kidnapped Holly from the airport. In broad daylight. That fucker has no fear."

A nod which shows my brother has heard of Adam Bisset. "Why?"

"Why does a man usually kidnap a beautiful woman?"

"Occam's razor. The simplest answer is usually the correct one."

"There's something about the timing that bothers me. He's here in France selling information and weapons to a terrorist cell. The biggest deal of his whole goddamn life, and for some reason he gets on a plane and flies to the United States. Only to fly right back."

"I've heard he's a crazy son of a bitch."

"He is, but it makes me wonder—especially with her sister gone missing."

That earns me a sharp glance. This is the man that the US military was so reluctant to relinquish a few years ago. This is the man that world leaders hire to head up their protection details. "You think the sister's tied up in this somehow?"

"Apparently she's some hotshot travel influencer."

"Seems like someone could walk through a lot

of borders like that."

"I don't want to tell Holly until I know something more specific. She'll lose her shit."

"In other words, she'll stop letting you fuck her."

My hands pull into fists. "Don't talk about her like that again."

Liam lets out a quiet laugh. "Just wanted to know where we stand."

"That's where we stand."

"Well, the sister disappeared off the map two weeks ago. Looks like Holly made some noise calling the embassy, but no one knew anything. Whether she was involved or not, it looks like she might have met a bad end."

"I hope not," I say, my voice grim. For Holly's sake, I hope her sister is alive. And I hope she's not tangled up in some sinister terrorist plot. I don't think her sister is inherently evil. I remember a mischievous smile on a blonde girl from years ago. But she might have agreed to move messages for money. Any number of small tasks that would have embedded her in a dark organization. Adam Bisset doesn't care about causes, which makes him the most dangerous kind of criminal. He only likes money—and chaos.

"We can go to the embassy," Liam says. "Or I

have a safe house in Nantes."

"What kind of a safe house?"

"Off the grid completely."

"There are locks?"

An incredulous glance. "There's a state-of-the-art security system."

"I mean, there are locks from the outside?"

He freezes. "Excuse me?"

"You heard me."

"You're planning on kidnapping her."

"I walked out on my mission, walked out on my job, walked out on my whole fucking life so that woman in there wouldn't be raped. You think I'm going to stop now that we've had some fresh baked bread? I'm keeping her safe no matter what it takes."

"You do this, she might end up hating you."

"In every outcome she ends up hating me. I don't give a shit about that," I lie. "As long as she's alive. As long as she's safe. Understand? That's what you're signing up for if you help me. I don't give a fuck what happens to me. This woman lives."

My brother turns his face into the sun. "I wasn't there for you when I should have been. Don't know what happened after I left, but I'm guessing it was no fucking picnic."

"This isn't about the past."

He faces me with those familiar green eyes, the same ones our father had. "The hell it isn't."

For a second I think he knows about the museum, the Louvre, the diamond. That was my first undercover mission. It was a test to see if I could blend in with criminals well enough to survive. In the end the US government didn't care much about the Regent Diamond. They liked the French being in their debt. What I saved for them, what I recovered, wasn't usually diamonds. I was tasked with saving lives. How many people will die because I chose Holly?

"The past doesn't matter," I say, more firmly this time.

"I read the coroner's report, you know."

"A heart attack." That was the official cause of death for our father. The coroner was too busy fucking his secretary to notice the petechial bleeding. Or maybe he was distracted by the way my father's mangled body had become bloated in the lake.

"Convenient," my brother says.

"Convenient?"

"That it happened right before you left for basic training."

"Right. So I could attend the funeral."

"Of course, that's what I meant."

In this conversation my brother accuses me of killing our father. And he forgives me for it. If anyone would understand the causes, it's him. Even so, he would think I was fighting back after my father was in one of his rages. The truth is my father was stone-cold calm when I approached him. I wanted him fully sober and aware when I beat the life from him. I wanted him to know I was doing it for my mother. Something happens when you kill a man in cold blood, even a murderer, even someone who deserves it. You lose a little piece of your soul.

My brother's green eyes are knowing. And hell, he would know. Rumor has it the man was an assassin for the US government. He knows all about killing people in cold blood.

"A nice family reunion," I say, my voice dry.

"Very nice. You're probably going to get dishonorably discharged."

"If I'm lucky. They might send one of you after me."

"Anyone touches you, they answer to me." My brother claps me on the back. "Once the military kicks you out on your ass, you should come join the family business."

"That a job offer?"

"We have safe houses in every major country. With locks on the outside. Consider them a perk."

CHAPTER TWENTY-THREE
HOLLY

LIAM DIDN'T COME alone. There's a driver wearing a black T-shirt and cargo pants, who I suspect is as dangerous as either brother. I take a deep breath in the backseat, finally feeling safe from the kidnapping. It's only been a few days, a week, of captivity, but I feel fundamentally changed. I'm some other being now. Not fully human. More animal.

I don't admire the sweeping hills of lavender. I'm too grateful for the comfort of leather seats and air-conditioning. How quickly I learned not to take them for granted.

Elijah and I are both sitting in the back seat, but there's a new distance between us. Even in the farmhouse, with the strangers who owned it, we felt close.

Now the real world has intruded.

"You must be eager to get back to the church," I say, hoping he'll open up to me.

Maybe it doesn't matter to him, what we shared. Maybe he has sex with a woman on every mission, but it matters to me. It feels like we're going to say goodbye.

"Yes," he says.

"And report to your lieutenant corporal."

"Lieutenant colonel," he corrects, almost absently.

"I hope he's not really angry with you. Maybe if I talked to him—"

"Absolutely not."

"I could explain that you had no choice."

"But I did," he says, gently now. He reaches over and squeezes my thigh, a touch that's both comforting and intimate. "I made my choice, and I have no regrets."

I want to ask what that means, but I'm aware that we have company only a few feet away. "We're going to Paris, right? I have to go to the embassy."

"We're going to Paris, and I'll find your sister."

Something about his word choice makes my eyes narrow. "By that you mean, you're dropping me off at the embassy when we get there, right?"

He sighs. "I didn't want to tell you this, but you can't go to the embassy. There's a red notice circulating that you're wanted for questioning by Interpol. My brother has connections into the agencies through his security firm, and he found it."

"What?"

"It means that Adam Bisset made it out of that basement. I'll handle him."

"I don't understand what that means. How are you going to handle him? Am I going to be arrested? I'm just a children's book author, and now I'm wanted by Interpol. Why do you look so calm?"

He doesn't look calm. He actually looks faintly amused, the bastard. "Do you know that your voice is going supersonic right now?"

"I thought this was over."

His expression softens. "You don't need to worry. I'll keep you safe."

That certainty warms me, and I relax into the plush seats of the SUV.

The small plane is just as comfortable, with low lighting and deep leather benches.

A steward brings champagne, which makes me think of Reims. Elijah's green-gold eyes meet mine, and I know he's thinking of the same thing. I probably tasted like champagne at the cathedral when we kissed.

At the small airport where we land, another black SUV picks us up. Night falls without a single star this close to Paris. We take fast roads through shadowy streets. Finally we pull in front of a building with marble pillars and stone steps. The men get out first and do something with hand signals that mean I'm allowed to get out next.

Inside, a dark green marble floor spans the length of the entire hall. Chandeliers cast a serene light on dark wood paneling. Everything here speaks to luxury and comfort.

It's the exact opposite of the basement of the medieval church.

Elijah confers briefly with Liam, who directs us upstairs. A lot of these appartements were built in the same style, so it shouldn't be shocking that this place reminds me of the converted boutique hotel suite where I stayed with my sister all those years ago. There's a small sitting area with baroque furniture, a bathroom with a claw-foot tub, and a view of the Eiffel Tower.

Oh, and a single bedroom with a large bed for us to share.

My cheeks heat as I imagine sharing that bed.

Will we continue the affair the way we did at the farmhouse? It seems likely. And I'm very aware that I still feel faintly grimy. Even with the bath, I don't feel like myself. My legs need to be shaved, my hair needs a deep conditioning.

If we're going to make love again, I want to feel beautiful.

I peek into a wardrobe, wondering if there will be a robe or something. Instead I find a full rack of clothes with tags from Dior and Yves Saint-Laurent. The drawers are full of lacy bras and silk panties. All of it new. "Whose clothes are these?"

"Yours," Elijah says, leaning against the doorframe, watching me.

I pick up something black and slender, blushing when I realize it's a thong. "How?"

"Liam had the place stocked for us."

"This is…" I make an embarrassed gesture. "Too much." My books pay me enough money. I can afford my modest home and my modest car. I can impulse buy at Target with the best of them, but that doesn't mean I can afford an entire wardrobe of designer clothes. It also doesn't mean I'd look good in them. It would be like watering a weed.

"I told Liam I'd pay for it already, if that's what you're worried about."

"These clothes won't fit me."

"The size?"

"No, the style. They're too fashionable."

He quirks an eyebrow. "You're not fashionable?"

"They're too… sexy."

He strolls past me and digs through the drawers. He comes up with something in a deep red with lines of black. I barely know what they are when he hands them to me, but they aren't heavy or hefty enough to cover me completely. "I want to see you in this."

His lids are heavy, as if he's already imagining me in the clothes. I risk a glance at his black cargo pants, where his erection presses against the fabric. That gives me enough courage to slip into the bathroom. I turn the sterling silver faucet all the way to hot and let the water scald me. I shave and scrub and lotion every inch of my body, until I feel like I've shed an entire layer of myself. Maybe mermaids are like snakes. Maybe they shed their skin to heal.

Steam fills the bathroom when I finally open the door and step out. The red and black bustier he chose for me pushes my breasts high. The matching panties dip low, barely covering my sex. I feel exposed and… fashionable. And sexy.

Maybe it's as simple as clothes that make a

woman feel beautiful.

Except, no. It's the way he's looking at me. Elijah must have found a separate bathroom and a separate wardrobe, because he's shaved and showered. He sits back on an armchair, his legs spread wide as if he's the king of all he surveys. In this Parisian suite, perhaps he is.

Our coupling in the forest was wild.

Our sex in the farmhouse was intimate.

Will this one feel safe and comforting, as luxurious as our surroundings? His hands roam my hips and thighs with blatant ownership. Then his hands curve around my ass. He touches me in my most private place, the place between my butt cheeks.

"Have you ever been taken here?" he asks, his voice low and hypnotic.

"No," I whisper.

He strokes me there, a casual brush of fingers. It's more sensitive than I would have thought. Connected by a straight line to my pussy. I clench around nothing, wanting his touch in a different place. "Tell me what you like, sweetheart. Besides getting fucked on your hands and knees in the mud. I know you liked that."

My cheeks must be on fire, but I can't deny that I'm wet. I feel the dampness, and it embarrasses me, even as I hope he finds it, hope he knows how much I can't resist. "I don't really know. Is that dumb? I haven't really... that much."

Amusement lances through his green eyes. "Haven't really what? Had sex? Fucked? Been eaten out? Do you like it when a guy goes down on you, Holly?"

I shake my head, unable to meet his eyes. "It's awkward."

There were a few attempts in college, and after I graduated, one boyfriend who worked at the coffee shop where I wrote. Which meant I had to find a new coffee shop once we broke up. The whole thing had always seemed like more trouble than it was worth—something I did to please the men in my life, but not something I enjoyed on my own.

A low laugh. "Fuck awkward."

He lifts me suddenly, pushing me forward until I'm on all fours, my knees on the warm cushion where he'd been lounging, my hands on the broad back of the chair. From this position I can see through the half window, through the breezy white curtains to the Eiffel Tower. It's lit up for the night, glowing like a beacon in the center of the city.

That's the position I'm in when he licks me from behind, when he bites my butt cheek. There's nothing awkward about the way he makes me moan. And that's the position I'm in when he fucks me, his cock in my pussy, his thumb in my asshole, riding me hard enough to make me grunt like an animal, fucking me until I scream his name to the starless night sky.

CHAPTER TWENTY-FOUR

ELIJAH

S HE COMES HARD enough that she almost passes out, and I carry her limp body to the bed. She curls around the pillow and falls asleep right away.

I stand at the edge of the bed, watching her, waiting. For what?

The urge to lie with her in my arms pulls at me. My hands flex as I imagine tangling them in her hair or holding her breasts. I don't only want her when we're having sex. I want to consume her every second of the day.

It's dangerous, this wanting.

Those iron bars in the church—they're still here, lined up around me like soldiers, keeping me from true freedom. Walking out of that basement did nothing to release me. I'll never be good enough for Holly—never soft enough, never kind enough.

So I turn around and leave the suite, where

my brother waits downstairs, sitting in an armchair like the one where I fucked Holly. I wonder if I looked the way he does now—so very alone.

At the bar I pour us both some Jameson, practically contraband in the land of wine and absinthe. It was our father's drink of choice, though he'd settle for beer when the liquor store cut him off and he had to go to the gas station. I sit across from him, setting down the glass. He glances at it a moment before taking a drink.

"First time I've had that in years," he says.

"Figured a family reunion should have some memories. Even if they're dark."

"I am sorry for—"

"Don't."

He runs a hand over his face. I recognize it because I do that, too, sometimes. I wonder if Holly and London share the same mannerisms like that. "I am."

"You don't even know what you're apologizing for."

"I know he was a sick fuck. And he was getting sicker. I left you to that."

"You protected me when you could." I remember my brothers taking beatings that were meant for me. I remember them giving me food at night when our father had passed out. I remember the way they protected me before they left.

"Since we're talking about it, did our mother—did she ever come back?"

"Hell."

"I looked for her. Later. When I had the resources. I'm not hoping for some big reconciliation, but if she needed money right now, if she needed—"

"She doesn't."

"Then it's true." He looks at me, his dark green eyes unfathomable. "She's dead."

I have to swallow hard against the memories. They're fleeting but all the more powerful because of being rare. Her singing a song. Her warmth when she held me. Feeding me. She must have lived in fear with that fucker as her husband, but she found love in her heart for us. "Yes."

He looks away, toward the window where the Eiffel Tower looks like a gaudy fucking party trick. I'll never be able to see it again without tasting Holly's sweet pussy.

The irony is, this was my first time in France since the diamond heist. And it's connected. Her being here isn't a coincidence. I involved her in my mission once before.

Now she's inextricably linked to this, too.

How will she feel when she finds out I used her—again?

"Having second thoughts?" Liam asks. "About keeping her here?"

Second thoughts? "Fuck no."

I knew when I walked out of that prison cell that she was mine. I probably knew even before that, when I first sensed an angel in there with me.

It's something deeper than affection. Darker than love. She's mine.

"Does she know that she's not allowed to leave?"

I shake my head once. "Not yet."

My brother cocks his head to the side. "If we had come from a different family, I might try to convince you not to do it this way. You could try talking to her, explain how you feel, explain what you're worried about."

It's like he's speaking a foreign language. "I'm keeping her alive."

"I have a feeling if I tried to take her from you, one of us would end up dead."

My whole body tenses. "You're not taking her."

"God, Elijah. He really did a number on us,

didn't he?"

"You seem pretty fucking normal." I'm the one too broken to even tell a woman I'm fucking that I care about her. I want her alive. That's the kindest sentiment I can offer. I'm basically a machine made to fight and lie and kill. There is no setting that allows me to love.

He takes a large swallow of scotch. "You have no idea."

"So tell me. You want me to work for your company? Tell me something about you that I could use to put you in jail. That's how you show you trust me. Mutually assured destruction."

"The sad part is how much logical sense that makes to me."

I take a sip. "I'm waiting."

He sighs. "I'm guardian to a little girl who... God, I've never even spoken the words aloud. I killed her father. Poison. One of those orders from the US government that they'd deny until the end. Only, I didn't know she was in the room. Didn't know she'd take a sip."

"Jesus."

"She almost died."

"And a judge thought you'd be a great dad?"

"Fuck no, but they were easy enough to bribe. I started taking care of her out of guilt, but now I care for her… because of herself. Who she is. Except she'll hate me if she ever finds out what I did."

"It's actually impressive how fucked up that is."

"Thanks," he says, his voice dry.

I hold out my drink. "To mutually assured destruction."

He matches my toast, and we both drink. He's right about one thing. Our father really did a number on us. We destroy the things we love, and then it's too late, far too late to fix them. When Holly finds out what I did, she'll despise me, but it won't matter then.

She's already mine.

CHAPTER TWENTY-FIVE
HOLLY

THE MONSTER IS back. Only this time, there's no leash. He's eating me, and I'm sobbing, begging for someone to help me. No one will help you. The words shimmer in the air, unspoken but understood. He gnaws on my body—skin, muscle, and bone. There won't be anything left of me. The monster pauses and looks up, his eyes flashing green and gold, and I scream.

"Holly."

I wake up screaming, the force of it sharp in my throat. The sound abruptly ends, and then I'm just shivering in the bed, Elijah's arms on my shoulders from where he shook me.

"There you are," he says with those same green-gold eyes.

"Sorry," I whisper.

"Don't apologize. You've just been through a trauma."

A trauma. Yes, I suppose that's what I've been

through. A white van. A dark hood. Every woman's worst nightmare. That's what happened to me, but it was only the beginning. There was a prison in the basement of a church. Attempted escape. Injuries. Pain. Fear. The entire thing feels like a nightmare, but I can't seem to wake up.

I sit up and settle the sheets around me, grateful for the small distraction. The window is cracked, letting in the faint sounds of the city at night. A car far away honks. Someone laughs. Music plays from some distant bistro.

"It's hard to believe I'm really safe. That I'm really free."

"You are. Adam will never touch you again."

"I can't stop thinking about Peter."

"He'll never touch you either."

"Because he's dead. We killed someone."

He makes a rough sound. "I killed him. And the only thing I regret is not killing Adam, too. I shouldn't have let you dissuade me. Now he's a loose end we have to clean up."

"How can I distance myself from what happened? I was there. I was in that cell, fighting him. I clawed his eyes. I keep remembering Peter's weight on me, and he'll never take another breath."

"And he'll never hurt anyone again. The

world is a better place for it."

"Who are we to make that call?"

"We are the people he hurt. We are the best people to make that call. You think some judge knows better than us? He would have hurt you if he could." Elijah pulls his shirt over his head. In the dim light I can see the scars on his back, the whip marks and the burns. The bruises are too dark to see without light. "He hurt me, too. Remember? I didn't only kill him for you."

"But you would have stayed," I remind him. "If it weren't for me."

"And probably died. I would have followed my mission to the grave if it weren't for you." He pulls me close to his body, wrapping me in his arms. The musk of him surrounds me. "So really, when you think about it, you saved my life."

"Shut up."

"I'm serious. I seem to recall that you wouldn't let it go by a certain lake. You wouldn't let me demur and not take credit for what I did. So you have to take credit, too. You saved me."

"Stop."

He dips his head and kisses me. It's coaxing and soft. It tricks me into kissing him back before I realize what I've done. "You. Saved. Me."

There's no winning this argument, so I press

myself into his arms, curling up like a small child. It's the middle of the night, and we're both awake. "Tell me a story."

"You're the writer."

"I know, but I need a distraction from the monsters in my head."

"Monsters?"

I nudge him. "Tell me something about you. Why did you join the military?"

"Same reason my brothers did, I assume. The only thing I knew how to do when I turned eighteen was fight. That's the place where you fight."

"But you got recruited to do the heist. That can't be normal."

"No, I was never normal. I scored off the charts on language processing, logical reasoning, spatial acuity, et cetera, et cetera."

That makes me sit up. "I thought you said the only thing you could do was fight. If your IQ is off the charts, then you can do a lot more than that."

He shrugs. "I always dumbed down my answers in school so that I would just get As and Bs. If you're the valedictorian or that shit, they expect more from you. Honor roll and speeches and going to college."

"What's wrong with college? I bet you could have gotten a scholarship."

"To do what? Become an accountant? Put money into a 401K? I never expected to live long enough to need a retirement. Joining the army was something I did to be useful. But no matter what shit they threw at me, I kept surviving."

"Do you ever think about what you'll do next?"

"I never thought there'd be a next. I never thought I'd live long enough to have one. If it happens, then I'm probably going to work for my brother."

"Is that what you want to do?"

"Life has very little to do with what I want."

What a different upbringing he had. So toxic and destructive. It made him feel like he can't seek happiness. It made him think he wouldn't even live very long. I wish I could go back and hit his father for doing this to him. I wish I could go back and save his mother. I can't do anything to change the past, but I have the man here with me in the present. I wrap him in my arms and pull him close. He lets himself be drawn into my embrace.

"Give me one dream," I murmur. "An impossible dream. Something you want."

"That's easy," he says. "You."

Confusion mars my brows. "I'm right here, Elijah. I'm here."

"Don't argue," he says, mirroring the words he once told me when we were being held captive under the church. "Don't fight. Understand? That will only make it worse."

"You're not still trapped. You're not still there."

"Aren't I?" he asks, and I shiver in the cool night air.

CHAPTER TWENTY-SIX

ELIJAH

THE SAFE HOUSE consists of three stories. The bottom one contains the traditional servants' quarters, and it's only accessible from the back of the house. The middle level is where the common areas are—the living room, the dining room, and a modest library. Modest in terms of size. It has original and signed editions from Balzac and Proust.

The top level has the bedroom. Bedroom, singular.

The entire place is designed for a single person or couple to use.

Unlike many of the flats in Paris, there's no balcony. Presumably that made this place useful as a safe house. There's also bulletproof glass and lead-filled walls to block signals passing through. Those things are easily disguised. As far as Holly knows, this house has an upgraded security system, but it's otherwise normal.

The next morning I find her standing at the window, drinking a cup of espresso as she watches the Eiffel Tower. Her face is more slender than it was when she was young, more haunted.

Especially after her time in captivity.

I should be returning her to her regular life.

She could be on a plane to the United States with a security contingent from my brother's company. So why isn't she? The thought of being separated from her feels like a grate running across my internal organs. I'm not sure what to call my feelings for her—obsession?

Being held in that church changed the internal makeup of my cells.

In a way, Adam succeeded in his goal.

He wanted to bring us closer together so that I would share the location of the diamonds. Or barring that, use her as bait for her sister. He did manage to fuse me to her in an elemental way, but I'll be damned if I let her be used as bait.

She turns when she sees me and smiles. My heart clenches.

How long will she continue to smile at me? She won't be pleased to see me anymore when she knows I'm keeping her against her will.

"I've been thinking," she says, planting a kiss on my lips, "about my last message from London."

I keep my voice even, not showing how important this is. "Oh yeah?"

"She said she'd been walking down memory lane, seeing some of the same stuff we saw when we were here as kids. So maybe she went to the Louvre. She's never loved art much, but there's plenty of great photo opportunities. I've seen her do the thing where she mimics a statue."

I've already checked London's Instagram account. There are no photos from her time in France. "Or maybe she went to Reims."

Her brow furrows as she considers this. "Maybe."

I have a different idea of what London meant by memory lane, but I can't share that with Holly. Not yet. "What else did she say about her trip? Did she share an itinerary?"

"Nah, she didn't like to travel that way. She'd drive to the airport and fly standby. Or go to the train station and buy a ticket for whatever was the next train. A free spirit."

Or fucking crazy. "Did she have a favorite hotel?"

"She never stayed at the same place twice. She said it was a waste of a trip to do the same thing."

Which makes her hard to track. And the clock

is ticking, both for London and for Holly. "Okay, then was there anything she hadn't seen in Paris that she wanted to see?"

She shakes her head. "No—except, well, she did love the Catacombs. I think she goes there every time she's in Paris. I always give her a hard time about how it's gross."

I pull out my phone and scroll to her account. Way down from last year there's a photo of her standing in the Catacombs with bones on either side, no one else around. "Who takes these photos?"

A shrug. "London's always attracting Insta-gram boyfriends. Guys who will follow her around taking pictures. Or maybe it's someone who works there."

"No, look. It's empty. You don't see it like that during a regular tour."

"You think she—what? Broke in?"

That makes me smile. "I meant, maybe she got someone to let her in off hours. But I like the way you think, sweetheart."

She blushes. "Well, I wouldn't put it past my sister, but she means well."

I'm not so sure about that, but I know that Holly loves her sister. And I can even understand it. I would probably kill anyone who looked at

Liam sideways, and I've only known him a few hours. Holly's been close with her sister her whole life. "It's a long shot, but we can go ask around. And while we're there, we can visit the Catacombs. I've never been."

A shudder. "I've never been either... on purpose."

"You don't like human bone architecture?"

"Sure, I like it. When it's making the human body. Not walls in a dark tunnel."

"You know... there's something reminiscent of your tooth fairy with her room made of teeth, her house bricked with teeth, the street paved with teeth."

That earns me a glare. "This is totally different."

"Aren't teeth made of the same thing as bones?"

Her lips quirk. "Fine. It's a little bit different. And I'll go in there, but only for my sister."

I pull open the wardrobe and find a black-and-white dress with spaghetti straps, low cleavage, and a flowy pleated bottom. She will look fucking edible. "Wear this," I say, handing it over.

She raises her eyebrows but accepts the dress. "Are you this bossy with all your girlfriends?"

SKYE WARREN

The word makes my chest constrict. Girl-friend? I've definitely never had one of those before. I've fucked women—efficiently, ruthlessly. But yes, if she is my girlfriend, I like deciding what sexy dress she will wear. Other men will want her body, but only I will get to taste her.

"Yes," I say because I'm this bossy with her.

She rolls her eyes, which I also like. As long as she wears the dress.

When she comes out of the room, she does a twirl for me. Then I'm on top of her, feasting on her milky skin and biting her tits. There's no way she can leave the safe house like this. I mark every inch of exposed skin and fuck her until her eye makeup looks like a dark mess.

She's even more beautiful this way.

Then she changes into a pale pink sweater dress and washes her face, making her look incredibly innocent. I almost, almost have to fuck her again. She tests my control at every stage. But it's worth the restraint when we step outside the safe house. She takes a deep breath.

Waning sunlight gives her skin an orange wash. And I know in this moment that the nightmare is miles away from her. In this moment she thinks she's safe.

CHAPTER TWENTY-SEVEN

HOLLY

T HE NEXT DAY dawns bright and sunny, and I feel almost hopeful about our situation.

We didn't find any clues at the Catacombs. The people who worked there swore they'd never seen her, and they had no idea how the photo on her feed was taken. But we're free and safe and healthy. A million miles away from the cold prison cell.

I find Elijah in the sitting area with a cup of coffee and a laptop open. He tilts it slightly toward me when I sit down beside him so that I can see what he's doing. There are a few chat windows open, where I can see him making inquiries into the location of London Frank.

He taps one that hasn't responded. "I have high hopes for this woman. She's the best hacker I know. And expensive. If your sister has any digital footprint, she'll find it."

"And if she doesn't?" I ask, worried.

His expression gentles. "She will. I'm sure of it. And while I'm waiting for an answer, we have lunch with my brother before he goes back."

"Goes back?"

"To the States. He has a… daughter, I guess you could say. An adopted daughter."

"Oh, that's sweet."

"Right," he says in a strangled tone. "Sweet."

"So have you met his girl?"

There's a weighted pause. "No. In fact I hadn't seen my brother in years. Since before we met."

"I thought that might be the case," I say, touching the back of his hand. He's helping me find my sister; I want him to know that I'm here for him, too. He may have his brother physically, but he's been without a family emotionally for a long time.

He stands, pulling away from me in a brusque manner. "Listen, while we're looking for London, I also need to wrap up loose ends with my commanding officer."

"The diamonds," I say, and he stops.

"What did you say?"

"I remember Adam asking where they were."

"Right," he mutters.

"You said you didn't know, but you do know,

right?"

He narrows his eyes at me. "Are you some kind of human lie detector?"

"No." I give him a shy smile. "I think it's just you that I can read."

A knock at the door interrupts us, and we look down the stairs to where Liam peers up. "Lunch is ready if you two are hungry."

Lunch turns out to be homemade ratatouille from a woman who lives onsite. I break the crusty bread to mop the delicious liquid and spices. I think I'm still feeling a little starved from going for days with very little food. When I can finally come up for air, I tell Liam, "I heard you have a daughter. What's her name?"

He glances at Elijah with an unreadable look. "It's Samantha. She's a violinist."

"Does she play at school?"

"Not really. She's a prodigy. She's played for the queen."

"Wow. That's incredible."

"Yes," he says, looking somewhat more at ease now. And very proud of this Samantha. "She's an incredible talent. Once-in-a-generation kind of thing."

"I'd love to hear her play."

His smile gets more reserved. "She doesn't

perform much these days."

"I'm glad I got to see you before you go. I really want to tell you how grateful I am for your help. I know you were doing it for Elijah, and we're basically strangers, but I really do appreciate it."

He nods. "I'm only sorry I couldn't find your sister."

"You had short notice." I smile at Elijah. "He's going to help me."

"Don't—" Liam says, then stops suddenly. It's as if the word was torn from him against his will. It hangs in the air between us, harsh and foreboding.

"Don't what?" I ask softly.

"Yes," Elijah asks, his tone harder. "Don't what, brother?"

Liam's eyes meet mine, a deeper green than Elijah's, somehow less tortured, though it's clear they're both haunted by demons from the past. "Don't give up hope. You'll find her."

We see him off, and another black SUV takes him away.

One of his other men, someone named Carson Blum, stands guard at the door. A security system is required to open the door from both inside and out. Though it looks like a comfortable appartement, it's clear this is a very secure location. That makes me feel even more relaxed. Adam won't be able to find us, and even if he did, he wouldn't be able to get in.

I watch from the window as the SUV pulls away. Then I turn back to Elijah, who remains at the kitchen table, watching me as he twirls a glass of wine. "Can we go check on those inquiries?" I ask, gesturing upstairs. "Maybe if they don't find anything, we can go to the embassy? Try to explain what happened, why there's a notice with Interpol."

He doesn't answer out loud, but he does stand and cross the room to me.

Something is strange about his mood right now. Ever since his brother said *don't*—in that strident, almost worried way. It seemed like he was going to say something else, something more cautionary than not to give up hope.

"I'm going out," he says, his voice gentle, as if he thinks I might object. "I'll find out what I can about your sister. Can you trust me to do that for you?"

"Of course." I put my arms around his neck. "I don't want to use your time when you're focused on your mission. I know this is a distraction."

"Everything about you is a distraction," he says, sounding frustrated, even angry, and then he kisses me, soothing away the sting. His lips offer regret and apology. His kiss promises to care for me even as he holds himself apart. "Carson is going to stay here with you."

He enters a long code quickly, and the door latches open. Then he's gone, and the security system beeps to let me know that it's active. I wander into the living room, where Carson stands at attention. He gives me a very official-looking nod, and I wave back.

I go back upstairs, hoping to see if someone has responded to one of his inquiries, but of course the laptop is locked. Instead I wander around, touching a small figurine of a dairymaid on the carved fireplace mantel. It would be nice to have a phone, to at least call my parents and let them know I'm okay. They know my sister well enough not to be surprised when she doesn't answer for a few weeks, but my mom and I have a call every Friday like clockwork.

It was too much to hope that this place would be luxurious and fully complete with a wardrobe for me and have a phone or laptop for me, but I make a mental note to ask Elijah about it when he gets back. Plus, now that I'm safe again, I'd like to start writing.

In the shallow drawer of a desk I find a pad of paper and a pen.

It's been years since I wrote any of my books this way, but needs must.

Ruby Crouch had seen hundreds of families flow through the front parlor. Some were angry, still in denial about their visit. Others sobbed their goodbyes. Mrs. Crouch guided, comforted, and issued dire warnings—whatever was necessary to ensure enrollment.

The School for Ordinary Girls was not an ordinary school.

This particular family had an air of mourning. There were two children. Only one was eligible to attend. She sat on the armchair in a new dress and patent leather shoes, her feet hanging a few inches above the floor.

Her mother insisted she was a good child, that she always obeyed the rules, that she was kind and good and smart. The room trembled. Her father made threats about what good treatment he required of her. The fire in the fireplace hissed sparks. Her older sister simply cried silent tears that matched the rain outside.

Then it was time for them to leave.

They went down the steps and climbed into their car and drove away. The little girl ran to the window to watch the taillights turn blurry and fade away.

"Come along," Mrs. Crouch said, for she had learned that it was best for children to become acclimated to their new environments sooner rather than later. "Your room is waiting."

This is where the child belonged.

Her mother could move the earth. Her father could change fire. Her sister, water. But this child had no special abilities. She was and always would be ordinary.

I sit back and shake out my hand, which isn't used to writing so much so fast. There's a lurch in my stomach as I study the words I've written. Every story has small pieces of me—what I ate for dinner and how I feel about willow trees. But the characters are made up. The world is made up. And yet I can't deny the similarities to this family and mine.

Even the parlor where they sat reminds me of the room I'm in. The rain-beaten window looks like the one here. I can almost imagine the Eiffel Tower existing in my story.

Which is ridiculous, for so many reasons. The girl in the story is trapped in the school. She has no options, no way out. I wasn't left here by well-meaning parents.

This is a safe house. I'm here by choice.

CHAPTER TWENTY-EIGHT

ELIJAH

LIEUTENANT COLONEL MARK Jefferson is waiting for me at the embassy.

His face is already red. He's evicted some poor diplomat from their office so he could sit behind a desk which has photos of someone else's family. Two privates stand at attention on either side of him, props that he uses to emphasize his power. They're also there to make sure I don't kill him if he pushes me too far. It's a perverse sign of respect that he knows I might.

He gives me a dressing down that would reduce a greener soldier to tears. I'm a disgrace to my country, disgrace to my rank, disgrace to my family. He doesn't even know if I have a family. He moves on to threaten me with a court-martial. He'll strip my rank and put me in jail.

"Yes, sir," I say when he takes a breath.

Then he gets to the good stuff.

He'll have me killed. He'll have me disappeared. No one will find the body. One of the privates widens his eyes. Surprise. That means he's new to this detail. Which means he'd be the first person I'd attack if I wanted to take Jefferson down.

I don't. At least not until I find out whether he's a danger to Holly.

"I built you up from nothing," he says, spit flying from his mouth. "You were worthless, you were nobody, and I picked you out of the dregs and made you into someone."

"Yes, sir." He's not wrong. The mission at the Louvre was his first test of my abilities. The rest of my career has been spent outside France. When we heard about an arms deal going down in Paris involving diamonds, it made sense to bring me back in. I had some old contacts here. As far as they know, I'm a punk kid from the US with an eye for shiny stones.

Jefferson narrows his pale, watery eyes. Everything about him is pale—his skin, his hair. He looks like a washed-out version of someone. "Tell me what happened."

At the beginning I can be completely honest. "As my last drop reported, I infiltrated Adam's operation as the person to handle the diamonds. They were selling guns to Africa and being paid in diamonds, which would need to be sold for cash in order to split the money."

"Go on."

"We hit a snag when we were visiting a contact of mine in Stalingrad. Adam insisted on coming with me, I think because he still doubted my loyalty. I was spotted by someone who knew me from my last mission in Paris."

"A Frenchman?"

"No, actually. An American. A travel Instagrammer."

"A what?"

"A civilian," I say, casting a quick glance at the privates by his side. I don't know whether he's already revealed how little he cares about the lives of random civilians.

"His name?"

"London Frank. She approached me separately and asked for money in exchange for silence. I think she believes I'm involved in another museum heist."

"So you neutralized the threat."

I didn't kill her. "I paid her."

He grunts. "Go on."

"Adam found out and thought I was skimming profits from the operation. He had his men lock me up. They tortured me for information."

One of the private's does a fast blink. The cigar burns are visible on my neck even when I'm fully clothed. The man must be new. It makes me want to wrap him in cotton and send him back to his mother, if he has one.

"Then I get a call from you saying you're in Paris. And for me to come. You summoned me, boy. No one summons me."

I refrain from pointing out that he did, in fact, come. "They kidnapped a woman. Another American." This is where the truth becomes dicey. If Jefferson knows that Holly's connected to London, to the diamonds, he'll demand custody of her. "I think Adam liked her, but I couldn't let her get beaten or raped. So we escaped through the countryside and came here."

"Let me get this straight, North. It was your mission to stop the sale of guns to a hostile country and to take custody of those diamonds for the US government. And now you're telling me you left without doing either of those things."

"Yes, sir."

He's back to being red in the face. Idly I wonder how close he is to a heart attack. It would simplify matters if he would only drop dead. "I assume you have a plan for completing your mission, or you will face my wrath."

"Yes, sir."

"And that is?"

"He wants the girl, sir. I have her."

"You'll use her as bait. When does this operation take place?"

I would never use Holly as bait. I want her as far away from this mess as possible, but I need for Jefferson to believe I'm cooperating. "Adam is injured. His main contact for the arms exchange is dead. I killed him before I left. He needs to sell the diamonds."

"You're my best man, North. I won't lie to you, because you're too smart not to realize it yourself. But that doesn't mean you're irreplaceable."

"Yes, sir."

"You want to fuck this girl they put in the cell with you? Don't deny it. I can smell the sex on you. I can see it in your eyes. I didn't hold on to a weapon like you without understanding how it works. You want to fuck someone, that's fine. You think anyone's going to believe her? No. You do what you need to do, but you damn well complete the mission."

Sometimes I wonder how we ever believed ourselves to be the good guys. Was I ever so disillusioned as to believe we were on the side of right? "Yes, sir."

"The arms deal may have already gone south. I can stop that on the other end if I have to. But the diamonds are here in Paris. It's our job to retrieve them using whatever means necessary. They're evidence, understand? They're essential. Your mission isn't over until you have them."

Spoils of war. "Yes, sir."

CHAPTER TWENTY-NINE

HOLLY

C HARLIE STUDIED THE swooping graph on the sheet. Calculus, it was called. As an ordinary child, she needed to learn how the world worked. She was not born knowing. She was not born being able to manipulate it. There was something written in the margin of her textbook. Numbers. Notes. She traced the handwriting with her pencil hovering over the page. It felt less lonely to know that someone had held this same book and learned this same math language.

She hopped down from the chair, which was too tall. And crossed the room to the window, which was also too tall. If she pushed up on her toes, she could see over the sill to the empty road. "They aren't coming back, Charl," she whispered.

She climbed the chair again and turned the page of her textbook. More swooping graphs and long formulas. More notes handwritten in the margins.

And the words, I know how to make magic.

A car door interrupts my writing, and I cross the suite to see Elijah emerge from a black SUV. He doesn't glance up to see me, only strides into the front door. I imagine him greeting Carson, who will tell him we had a quiet dinner of bread and cheese while he was gone.

Footsteps climb the stairs, and I run to meet Elijah.

He looks more tired than when he left, but I imagine anyone would be after a twelve-hour day. There are lines on his face, shadows in his hazel green-gold eyes.

"Are you okay?"

A small smile curves his lips. "I should be asking you that."

"I'm fine," I say a little too brightly, glossing over the fact that I bit my nails, paced the room, and peppered poor Carson with questions about his life for way too long. I'm basically bursting with emotion right now. "Did you find out anything about my sister?"

"Not yet, but I should have answers from my contacts online." He grabs his laptop from the coffee table and settles on the sofa. I curl up beside him, marveling at how natural this feels. The way it would be if a boyfriend and girlfriend were looking up movie times. Instead we're looking up who might have harmed or kidnapped my sister, but still.

When he logs in, the little chat window blinks.

No info yet, says the message. *Wire the money to continue search. 1M.*

Something sharp twists in my stomach. "One M," I say, reading the end of the message aloud. "What does that mean? Is it her signature? A way of signing off?" My guesses seem unlikely, but I'm holding out hope.

"No, it's an amount."

Another twist of the knife in my stomach. "One million. One million dollars?"

"Euros, actually. Don't worry about it."

"Of course I'm worried about it. This is my sister, and someone's demanding one million euros for information about her. Is this a hostage situation? What's going on?"

"Relax," he says, which has the opposite effect on me. "She's not being held hostage. This woman, this hacker is providing a service, and I'm paying for it."

"Listen, I understand that you are richer than me. I get that. And I understand you're helping me here, but there's something off about this." I stand and stride away from him. "I just need to stop and make sense of this for a second. You're not even blinking an eye at paying one million euros for information. What if it's not even her? What if it doesn't lead to her?"

"It will."

"How do you know?"

"Because the hacker backs up her information."

"I don't understand why we even need a supersecret, superexpensive hacker to find my sister. Something is going on here, and I don't understand."

He flicks a few keys on the laptop—no doubt wiring one million euros, before shutting the lid. Then he stands and approaches me, hands out, placating. "Listen. You don't need to worry. I promised you I would find her, and I will."

Tears prick my eyes, and I press my palms against my sockets to hold them in. "Look, if we have to pay money to get her back, I'll do it. I'll mortgage my house or ask my parents or something. I don't know. But we can't owe you this kind of money. I can't owe you this."

"You don't owe me anything."

He seems so serious, so sincere. I want to fall into his arms and believe everything. Except things that I accepted in that prison cell don't make as much sense in the clear light of day. I walk away to the window, to the beautiful view of the Eiffel Tower, only now there's fog blocking the sight. "It's quite a coincidence, isn't it? Me ending up in a prison cell with you."

"Holly."

"Except it's not a coincidence, is it? I don't understand it, but it's not."

"Don't do this. Nothing good will come of you asking me these questions."

"The truth will come from asking these questions."

He gives me a sad smile. "The truth has never been anything good for me."

I know he's talking about his mother and her death at the hands of his father. I know he's talking about the family secrets that nearly strangled him, but I need to know. This is my family at stake. "Why did I end up in that prison cell with you?"

"I don't know."

It feels like one of those half-truths. "Why do you want to find my sister?"

"Because you asked me to."

It's not a matter of finding the right answer. It's about finding the right question. I look down, and then I know. "Where are the diamonds,

Elijah?"

"Fuck, Holly."

"Where are they?"

"You, too? It's not enough I had Adam hounding me."

"Where are the freaking diamonds?"

"They're with your sister. Is that what you wanted to know? She saw me in Paris and recognized me from Reims. I stashed them on her, the same way I once stashed diamonds on you. It's becoming a habit with you Frank girls."

"Where did you really go today? Were you even looking for her?"

"I reported to my commanding officer."

Hurt burns like acid down my throat. He may not have owed me his time, but he sure as hell didn't have to lie about it. And it sounds like she's some kind of enemy of the US government right now. Is she in danger? That wouldn't have happened if he hadn't given her diamonds. He's using her the same way he used me all those years ago. We're nothing but props to him. Mules to carry things he needs moved around. Pawns on a chessboard.

He leans forward, setting his elbows on his knees. "Where's your sister?"

"I don't know," I cry, my voice rising, panic a

fist around my neck. "Isn't that what I've been telling you? Isn't that why I came to Paris?"

"Or maybe you came to run away with her and a fortune's worth of diamonds."

"I don't want diamonds; I don't care about diamonds. They mean nothing to me." I'm going supersonic again, but I can't stop. "I only want my sister."

"Find one, and we find both." Those green eyes flash. "And we will find both."

"This is crazy," I whisper, feeling like a cornered animal. Feeling like the hair at the back of my neck is raised in warning. My sister isn't the only one in danger. If she's an enemy of the US government, so am I. I want to lash out, but I know I'd lose that fight.

"I promise you'll be safe," he says.

He's lying. I feel like throwing up that baguette and gruyere from earlier. I stand and head down the stairs without saying a word. The whole world looks surreal, underwater.

"Holly," he says, his voice too close for comfort.

"Leave me alone."

"Holly, you can't go out there."

I whirl on him, incredulous. "What do you mean?"

"You understand. It's not so different from the place where we were."

"The place where we were had iron bars. And a lock. And rats, probably." I make a sweeping motion to the opulence and comfort of the safe house. "It's nothing like this."

"Except in one way. You can't leave."

"Why not?"

He looks away, as if overcome with some emotion. But when he looks back at me, there's no feeling whatsoever in his green eyes. He might as well be a machine. "Because I won't let you."

Walls close around me. Iron bars lock into place. They've been there all along, only I couldn't see them. This is a prison the same as the church. In both places I was kept by a man who thought I was an object. Not a person. Bile rises in my throat.

I run toward the door, expecting to hear Elijah's footsteps thundering after me, expecting his strong arms to catch me. But I reach the door with no problem, only to be confronted with a black screen. I don't know the code. I don't know freaking the code. The handle doesn't even turn. The door doesn't open. The alarm system that I thought kept me safe is keeping me captive.

"Let me out," I say.

He approaches me with caution, like you would a wild animal. That's how I feel. It's probably how I look, my hair and eyes gone crazy. "It's not safe for you out there."

"Says you, but here's the problem. I don't believe a word you say."

"I'm not lying to you."

"That's exactly what liars say."

His lips twitch, the bastard. "Listen. I'm keeping you safe, and I'm going to find your sister. That's exactly the situation we were in an hour ago, and you weren't pissed at me then."

"That was before I knew you were using my sister in some kind of dangerous mission."

"She involved herself."

"And she's just going to hand over the diamonds? No one's going to hurt her?"

"That's up to her."

Oh God, London. Where are you? "I don't care. Let me go."

"That's not going to happen."

I glance over Elijah's shoulder to where Carson stands at attention. His gray eyes meet mine. "You," I say, desperate now. "Please help me. He won't let me leave."

"I'm sorry, ma'am."

Angry tears flood my eyes. "You knew. All

along when we were talking about you and your nine siblings, you knew I was a prisoner here. Your mother would be ashamed of you."

He does look sober. "Yes, ma'am, but I work for Liam North."

Apparently working for someone means doing anything they ask, including kidnapping. How did I go from being an ordinary woman who wrote in a coffee shop to being torn between possessive, domineering men? I throw myself at Elijah, using both fists to beat his chest. It's pointless and maybe even mean, but I don't care. I'm trapped. Literally trapped, and it feels like I can't stay in one place. I can't even hold my body together, so I hit him. My fists bounce off his pecs, not even able to sustain a solid blow. "I hate you," I say, my voice breaking. "I hate you."

Those robot green eyes look back at me. "I never thought you would love me. I knew I would never deserve that, but I'm keeping you. I'm not letting you go."

CHAPTER THIRTY

ELIJAH

THAT COULD HAVE gone better.

When I enter the bedroom, I see that Holly has built a wall made out of pillows right down the middle of the bed. It reminds me of the old bolsters, a wooden board used to separate young people so their hands wouldn't wander during sleep.

"Holland Ashley Frank." I got her full name from the dossier Liam gave me.

She does not move.

"Holly. I know you're not sleeping."

"I hate you."

"We need to talk. The more you tell me about your sister, the sooner we can find her."

She sits up, making the wall of pillows spill over into my side of the bed. "Why would I tell you anything? I don't want you to find her. I hope she buys up all of Paris with those diamonds."

"Diamonds like that don't get sold at pawn shops. She starts flashing those around, someone is going to kill her and keep the black velvet bag."

She flinches. "And you're going to help? I don't believe you."

"I'm not going to help her sell them. I'm going to help her get out of the goddamn crosshairs."

"She's only in the crosshairs because you put her there."

I sigh, thinking back to that day when I'd seen London in the back alley. For a second I thought she was a prostitute. Then when I recognized her, anticipation beat in my chest. I hoped Holly would be with her. Of course she wasn't. They weren't teenagers on a family trip anymore.

Could I have scared London into keeping my secret without giving her anything? Maybe. Maybe not, but I wanted the link to Holly, God help me. That probably makes me fucked in the head.

I didn't know Adam was going to turn on me.

I also didn't expect to find Holly thrown into the cell with me.

"Holly. What is your plan here? Are you going to give me the silent treatment?"

She ignores this.

The pillows spill over like a fluffy white cloud. I pick up one of them and toss it onto the ground. Another. And another. Soon the bed is empty except for Holly's slender body, the sheet, and the pillow under her head. She turns resolutely away from me, her knees bent.

The loose sheet bunches in my fist, and I tug it away, exposing her pretty legs and sexy ass in a silk negligee. She makes a sound of surprise that goes straight to my cock.

There's absolutely nothing ugly in that wardrobe. Only the softest fabrics and the most expensive lines. She looks like a Victoria's Secret model and acts like a goddamn librarian.

It's a fantasy I never knew I had. Until her.

"I'm going to remove every single thing between us," I say.

She clutches at the silky fabric. "How dare you."

"Or you can tell me what I want to know."

"I don't know where she is."

"You know her better than anyone else. You can help me find her."

She glares at me. "Never. I'm never helping you."

I give her red silk an insolent once-over. "Then I'm afraid I'll have to take that."

She stands, and I brace myself to catch the furious body like before. I want her to beat my chest with her fists, not because it hurts, but because it makes me feel alive. Instead she lifts the black lace at the hem of her nightgown. Then she pulls it off.

I stare at her naked body, sweating even though I'm the one who initiated this. She's so goddamn beautiful. If she were only less pale, less pink, less perfect, then maybe I could think straight. She makes me want to do terrible things to her. She makes me want to wrap my hands around her neck and feel the moans in her throat. She makes me want to fuck her so hard she begs me to stop. She makes me want, want, want, and it's painful holding back.

What's the purpose of control?

What's it ever gotten me but another pointless mission?

"There," she says, her voice unsteady. "What will you do to me next? Throw me into a cell? Threaten me? Make me kiss you for a bottle of water?"

"I don't have to threaten you to get a kiss, sweetheart."

Her expression turns mutinous. Is it wrong that I'm hard as a fucking iron bar right now? I

DIAMOND IN THE ROUGH

want her fighting me. I want her turned on even as she wrestles with her morality. I want her to come so hard she's screaming my name even as she loses.

I grasp the back of her neck and pull her close. Her lips are pressed together in defiance. I press a kiss to them. It's like a brick wall. Another kiss. It's a very sad fact that I enjoy this even without her consent. I nibble her bottom lip, and she makes a growling sound.

Her palms push me away. "Why did you give her the diamonds?"

"So I could steal them."

"Bullshit," she says.

I stand up straighter. "Excuse me?"

She steps close enough that we're toe to toe, her bare breasts brushing against my chest, her eyes a foot away from mine. They're brown and luminous tonight, as if she's fully in her power. That's the irony of this little interrogation.

The more I question her, the more I need her.

"You heard me. And I know you're basically a genius, so you understand, too. Bull. Shit. You gave her the diamonds because you wanted to sleep with her."

For a moment I stare at her. And then reality hits me, and I burst out laughing.

This is the wrong thing to do. I know it's the wrong thing to do, but I can't help it. London Frank? She's fucking gorgeous, but she has nothing, not a single thing on my little tooth fairy with streets paved with teeth. She's vicious and authentic and raw.

Her hand rises. I have plenty of time to catch her wrist or step back, but I let the slap come. The sting makes my cock flex in my jeans.

She stares at her palm, which looks pink from impact. "I can't believe I just did that."

CHAPTER THIRTY-ONE

HOLLY

H E DOESN'T LOOK angry that I slapped him. He looks amused.

"Do it again."

I raise my hand, but the heat of the moment has passed. I'm not a violent person. My sister's life is at stake, and I don't know how to help her. I only know that I can't trust Elijah. He's been dishonest with me every second that I've known him. "No."

Disappointment flashes through his green eyes. "You're twenty-four years old and still worried about being upstaged by your sister?"

"I don't resent her for it, but I'm not blind either. She's beautiful."

He tugs me gently, and I find myself following him. It seems like my body trusts him even if my mind knows better. He pulls me in front of the dresser, where the mirror reflects me back at him. I have to admit that it's erotic, the way I'm completely naked while he's fully clothed, my softness against his hardness, my pale skin against his tanned muscles.

He reaches around and places two fingers at the hollow of my neck. "The way your pulse flutters here." His hand falls lower, to the place between my breasts. "The way your body dips here." His hand falls lower to the gentle curve of my stomach and my belly button. "The way you suck in your breath when you're about to come, like you're going underwater."

"What's your point?" I say, feigning bravado in the onslaught of sensuality.

His green eyes meet mine in the mirror. "You are beautiful."

He says the words so simply that I can't help but believe him.

It doesn't make him trustworthy in general. I may not be able to trust him with my life, or my sister's life, but I know that he finds me attractive. Maybe that's the appeal between us.

He lives a life of subterfuge. I mostly live in made-up worlds.

This chemistry between us, that's real.

"I'm going to spread your legs," he says, his voice thoughtful. "And then I'm going to fuck you. It'll be long and hard, so you should hold on tight. If I have to fuck you right into the ground, I will. If you're flat on the floor, I'll be there, pumping into you from behind."

My sex clenches, readying myself for him, even as my mind screams that this is wrong.

He kicks one of my legs apart with his booted foot. Then the other, so I'm spread wide. The feel of leather on my bare ankles makes me shiver. The sound of a zipper behind me gives me the last chance to change his mind.

"Elijah," I whisper. "This isn't how you want me."

It's not exactly an objection. It's a cautionary tale. He notches the head of his cock to my pussy, and I can't help but tilt my hips to take him better. "That's where you're wrong. I don't want a pretty girl to stay home and cook pancakes when I roll through town. I want hard. Fast. I want to hold you down and make you take my cock until you cry."

Large hands grasp my hips, and he thrusts into me. I'm wet but it still feels like a stretch to take him all the way to the root. My breath whooshes out of me, and I rise up on my tiptoes to escape the burn. He pulls out to the tip and then thrusts in again.

His lids are low across green and gold eyes.

"This is how I want you."

I meet his gaze through the mirror and shake my head. "You want me to submit to you, to give in, and I'm never going to do that, no matter how hard you fuck me."

Despite my best efforts at being cold, I flinch on the word *fuck*.

He pulls back and thrusts in hard, as if he took my words as a challenge. I wobble on my tiptoes and grasp the dresser for support. The whole thing wobbles ominously, but it holds, even when Elijah thrusts into me again, when he fucks me harder and faster, even when the emotion threatens to overwhelm me and tears prick my eyes.

Friction. That's what I tell myself. This is about science. Physics and biology conspiring to make me have an orgasm even though I don't want one.

"Elijah," I whisper.

And he stops. That's the horror of this moment, how solicitous he can be even as he breaks my heart. A dull flush darkens his cheeks. His hair is in wild disarray. "Am I hurting you?" he asks.

I want to say yes, but the truth is that my body aches for completion.

Awareness comes over his face, and it makes

him look smug. I hate him for this, but it makes him look hotter—the certainty that I want him, that I can't hate him quite enough.

He pushes in again. Friction, friction, friction.

My sex doesn't know this is wrong and messed up. The pressure builds, and then he reaches around and flicks my clit, and I climax, clamping down around his cock. He grunts. His fingertips dig into my hips, and he comes in three rapid-fire thrusts followed by a long hold.

He pulls himself out, and his come drips down the inside of my thigh.

My muscles feel shaky, unable to support me even as I remain bent over the dresser. I'm cold and sweaty at the same time, covered in cooling come. Elijah returns from the bathroom with a hand towel that he hands me, his gaze cold. I wipe between my legs, wondering what feels so different, so painful about this. He's taken me roughly before. And he made me come. It's after, I realize. He never held me after sex before now, so I shouldn't expect it now.

This time he didn't even undress fully. Now he zips up his jeans and stalks out of the bedroom. I hear him descend the stairs. Then I'm left alone with only my shame and my hurt.

CHAPTER THIRTY-TWO

ELIJAH

OVER THE NEXT three days I get exactly what I wanted. Holly gives her body without reserve, but she doesn't hold me in her sleep. She doesn't smile at me over coffee.

She doesn't tell me stories about fairies or mermaids or dragons.

It's basically hell.

I find myself longing for the days in the cell, when she would at least talk to me in the dark. If this is my punishment for involving her sister, for lying to her, it's working. But I'm not sure how I can fix it. I can't go back in time and take the diamonds back from London. I can't go back and tell the truth to Holly, not that I would have. That's the crux of the issue, really. She wants me to be some other man. An open book. That's not me.

Jefferson leaves messages every hour on my burner phone. I ignore him, but it's only a matter of time before he sends someone else in to fix this mess. Holly, though innocent in every way, is at the crux of the issue. She's the one who has access to London, which means Adam needs her. Anyone would realize that using Holly as bait is the cleanest way to fix this mess.

I won't let that happen.

Liam calls me on the fourth day. "I found something you might be interested in."

"Don't tell me someone was fencing a handful of rare diamonds on La Villette because I already heard about that. And questioned the owner of the pawnshop."

"By questioned do you mean kicked his ass? Because he's a son of a bitch."

Yeah, Clef Augustin is a dirty bastard who makes his money selling crack in secondary schools. I made sure to knock him out before I left, but that won't stop him. He'll be back on the street corner tonight. "It shouldn't be possible for a travel blogger to stay this invisible."

My brother has been helping me look for her from Texas using his contacts. "That's what I was thinking. So I started asking around about Adam Bisset instead."

Unease turns my stomach. "Don't trip the wrong wire, Liam."

"I'm careful. Anyway, apparently he's a golden boy at Interpol. Awards and honors, all that shit. No hint that he's done a damn thing wrong, except that he's missing."

I remember his fake French accent. "*Make her come*," he said. "*Make her come and you can have this.*" Then I remember Holly's voice, small and hoarse. "*I'm thirsty. Please.*"

He's a dead man. I promised to kill him, and I will keep that promise.

I let him live in a moment of insanity, but I won't make that same mistake again.

"What does Bisset have to do with anything?"

"Do you know that he went missing the same time you escaped? The cell phone you'd placed a tracker in went dark. Three of his men turned up dead."

"Hell. I guess he got spooked and decided to run."

"That's good news for the arms deal."

"The Russians will be pissed. Adam's made himself powerful enemies."

"What if he didn't go on the run alone?"

"You said he killed his men. Three. That's all of them. Unless... no. You mean London. That doesn't make any fucking sense."

"What if he used her to test your loyalties?"

"There's a flaw in your logic. Adam kidnapped Holly because he wanted to find the diamonds. Why would he do that if he already had them?"

"For leverage over London? Who knows?"

Holly comes downstairs, and I speak quietly, "I have to go."

"Be careful. I've only just found you. I don't want to lose you."

"You're just trying to protect your investment," I say. "Don't worry. I'm going to work for you."

When I hang up the phone, Holly comes over to me. She usually only comes down for meals, and then to eat in silence. We ate dinner a couple hours ago. I was about to go upstairs to sleep before my brother called.

"You were talking to Liam?"

"He has some theories about your sister."

"Do you swear that you'll keep her safe if you find her?"

I don't make promises lightly. When I swore to kill Adam Bisset, I meant it with every fiber of my being. I would come back from the grave to complete that. So I won't promise not to harm London until I'm sure she'll hand over the diamonds without a fuss. "No."

Tears swim in dark eyes. "She's my sister. Please."

She says *please* the same way she said it before, when she was held captive in a dank cell. *I'm thirsty. Please.* Adam Bisset was a monster for making her kiss me to get water. And I'm a monster for making her beg for her sister's life. "I'm sorry."

Her eyes close, and when she opens them again, there's a new resolve. "Then I'm asking that you sleep on the couch tonight. Not upstairs. Not in bed with me."

I want to refuse, to demand rights to her body, to demonstrate my mastery over her. If I can just make her come, I can prove how little her words mean. Except her words mean everything. If she denies me access to her pretty pink cunt, I don't have the will to force her.

"Holland," I say, my voice rough.

She shakes her head and turns away.

It feels like I'm losing something precious. Like holding a diamond and watching it dissolve into sand. I catch her before she returns upstairs.

I'm inches away from her.

"Hi," I say, desperately, half begging. Waiting for her to say, *hi back*.

Instead she turns and climbs the steps, her

DIAMOND IN THE ROUGH

shoulders down, her sobs like knives in my ears. This woman is crying because of me. I'm a dragon who flew her to the top of a mountain, far from the water she needs to breathe.

She should hate me. She does.

This is a war that neither of us will win.

CHAPTER THIRTY-THREE
HOLLY

*W*HEN SHE WROTE *the last symbol, all four pages of it, the desk shook.*

Such a small victory. Everyone else could make things move without having to work out the mathematical formula. Then again, everyone else wasn't ordinary. She had lived with her parents' disappointment for so long, this almost felt like a betrayal.

Why didn't they teach this in the School for Ordinary Children?

Her textbook contained regular formulas. Only in the margins could she find the ones that made magic. Not only for a single element. For all of them. According to whoever wrote the notes, she would eventually be able to accomplish it without actually writing them down. Thinking would be enough. That made her like her family, didn't it? She would get to go home.

The next page dashed her hopes.

Don't tell anyone, *the student wrote*. They don't want you to know.

This was strange. She was a disappointment to her family. A mark of shame. Why wouldn't they be pleased to find out she could make magic, too?

I put down my pen.

Elijah climbs the stairs. I turn my face toward the window, attempting to ignore him. It's like trying to ignore a hurricane while you stand in the middle of an open field. He batters my senses. I can feel, smell, taste every inch of his muscled body. Memory is a cruel companion.

He appears on the landing, and I spare a glance.

Black slacks and a white button-down. He looks dressed for a date. That's my first thought. Next I realize how ridiculous that is. This man doesn't take women on dates unless he's trying to steal diamonds back from them. "My contact came through," he says, his voice even. He doesn't seem affected by my animosity. He's still as pleasant as ever. "The hacker. She found traces of your sister in east Paris."

"What does that mean, traces?"

"A digital footprint."

"Can I come with you?"

A firm shake of his head. "No, I don't think I

could manage both Frank sisters. At least not without hurting you, and I refuse to do that."

"What a gentleman," I say, my voice dry.

He's already hurt me more than I would have thought possible. It seems like my heart would know better than to love a man who's a thief and a liar. The fact that he does those things in the name of the greater good doesn't make him any less dangerous to me. His methods don't take into account the emotions or safety of a regular person.

"I'm not your enemy," he says softly, but there's a soft lilt at the end of his low voice, as if he isn't sure of the truth of the statement. It's almost a question.

"You're not my friend."

"No," he agrees. "I'm not your friend."

I pick up my pen as if I'm going to write and stare at the words, unseeing. I don't know how to think when he's standing so near me.

"I'll be back tonight," he says, approaching me, and I tense.

He leans close and places a kiss on my forehead. It feels like a goodbye.

Then he's gone, taking his masculine scent and warmth with him. I'm left bereft, hating myself for wanting more of him, my body fighting the urge to run after him.

I touch two fingers to my skin where he kissed me, as if I can hold it in.

Low voices converse below.

He's talking with Carson, who I haven't spoken to since I found out I'm a prisoner here. It doesn't make sense to care about my captors. No matter how nice the cell.

There's a beep from the alarm as it disarms. A brief few seconds when I could actually escape. If I had the desire to jump out of a two-story window. If I could land without him finding me. If I had any money or resources or a place to go.

So I remain seated.

Or maybe those are only the excuses I tell myself. Maybe if the prison is warm and comfortable enough, the captive learns to enjoy herself.

I'm wearing a tiered Gucci dress in rustic floral patterns. It's like a runway version of what Marisol would wear in her real farmhouse.

I peek out the window in time to see the black SUV drive away. It's a sunny day. Down the street I see a couple strolling arm in arm. A young mother pushes a stroller. Such domesticity. Such contentedness as I'm trapped in this luxurious cell.

What would they do if I started banging on the window?

Most likely Carson would notice and stop me.

That's a depressing thought.

I wander back to the bedroom and lie down. It's something most people might not realize, the boredom of living in captivity. I lie down on the bed with its many pillows and remember the night Elijah threw them all to the floor. He took me against the dresser there.

It wasn't the last time we had sex, but it was the last time I expected it to be sweet.

"Pssst."

The sound is soft enough that I think I imagined it. Until it comes again.

"Pssssst."

I look behind me to the back window, which opens to an alleyway. A familiar pair of eyes peek over the sill. "London," I breathe before scrambling off the bed.

She's perched on the casement from the window below her, a very precarious situation that makes my heart swoop in fear. "Hey, Sis."

"What are you doing?" I whisper furiously. "Come inside."

Her head shakes. "No, you have to come with me."

"The diamonds. Do you have them?"

She hesitates. "Not here."

DIAMOND IN THE ROUGH

"You're going to fall," I say, my voice rising. Elijah was right to be worried. Right to think she wouldn't want to give the diamonds back. He was right, and everything is wrong.

"Don't go supersonic," she warns.

"I was so worried about you." I'm definitely going supersonic.

"Shhhh. Mr. Downstairs took a potty break, but he's not going to be there for long. We have to get you out before that happens." The window is already cracked, and she opens it wider. Ancient hinges emit a low-pitched groan. "Hurry."

"How did you disarm the alarm system?"

"You don't want to know. Come on, Sis. It's now or never."

There are a million reasons to stay where I am. Starting with a very healthy and normal fear of heights. The back of the house actually drops three stories. There's every chance I could fall to my death attempting to escape. Then there's Elijah. While I'm pissed at him, I believe he won't hurt me. Is that enough of a reason to stay?

In the end all my worry and deliberation is for nothing.

He may not be a danger to me, but he's definitely a danger to my sister. I would do anything for her. Including walk away from the captor that

I love.

"Scoot over," I say, and I see the relief in her dark blue eyes.

I climb down the drain in my expensive designer dress and ballet flats, slipping only once. We make it to the street where we fit into the crowd of couples and young mothers. We are two fashionable sisters exploring Paris—one of us carrying priceless diamonds, the other with absolutely nothing in her pockets, not a single euro.

By the time we are three blocks away, I'm sure we won't be found.

Ten blocks away, and my heart begins to hurt.

"London," I say, my heart still pounding from fear and grief.

"I know. It's fucking crazy. I got your messages, by the way."

"Then why didn't you respond?"

"It's a long story. And I didn't get them until after you were in France. Where did you go? I thought you'd try the embassy or something, but you disappeared."

Disappeared. That's one word for being kidnapped and held in a church's underground prison. "It's a long story, but first tell me what happened to you. Why did you stop replying?"

She takes my hand, and I squeeze back, still so relieved to have found her, safe and whole. "Mine is a long story too."

"Let me start it for you: Holly, I have really expensive diamonds."

"You know about that?" Her eyes twinkle. She shows me her left hand and flips a gold band around. The largest diamond I've seen in real life sparkles from the simple setting. "I'm engaged."

"What?"

She snorts. "Not really. It's just the most convenient way to keep it where people don't ask questions. Well, they do ask questions, but I've made up someone tall, dark, and handsome. He's a stock broker in New York. I can't settle on a good name for him, though."

We pass a shop with expensive china, its lights off. The front door says *sur rendez-vous uniquement* and underneath *by appointment only*. I pull my sister into the empty doorway of the store. "This is serious. Did you steal that?"

"Of course not. Someone gave it to me."

Lord. "I know you found the diamonds. I know Elijah stashed them on you."

Her expression falls. "Don't be angry at me."

"Why would I be angry?"

"Because when I saw them—I wanted to keep

them. That's why I went dark. That's why I stopped responding to you. It was the only way to keep the money."

"God, London. It's not that simple. They're not going to let it go. There are men after you. Not only Elijah. They want them back."

She twists the ring backwards again. Her fingers curl around the stone. "They're mine."

"They're not."

She closes her eyes. "Holly, I didn't want to tell you this, but I got mixed up with some bad people. I need the money."

Her fear shimmers in the air around us, and my heart clenches. I wrap her in my arms. "It's okay. We'll figure it out together now."

"You won't leave me?" She looks impossibly young—younger than me, right now.

She went on the run with millions of dollars in diamonds. That kind of hiding lasts forever. She'll never be free to post her photo online. I'll never be able to publish another book. "Do you know what you're asking of me, London?"

Everything. She's asking for everything that I am.

"I'm sorry." She looks stricken. And frightened.

My sister. She's my sister. "Of course I won't

leave you," I tell her, feeling as if I've just jumped off a cliff. I'm falling into the rocks headfirst, clutching diamonds in my fist.

THE END

Thank you for reading DIAMOND IN THE ROUGH! I hope you loved Elijah and Holly's story. Find out what happens when he catches her in GOLD MINE.

SIGN UP FOR MY NEWSLETTER to find out when new books release!
www.skyewarren.com/newsletter

Join my Facebook group, Skye Warren's Dark Room, for exclusive giveaways and sneak peeks of future books. And Elijah's brother Liam has a book, too! If you haven't read Liam's story yet, be sure to pick up OVERTURE…

Liam North got custody of the violin prodigy six years ago. She's all grown up now, but he still treats her like a child. No matter how much he wants her.

"Swoon-worthy, forbidden, and sexy, Liam North is my new obsession."

– New York Times bestselling author
Claire Contreras

Keep reading for an excerpt from OVERTURE…

✧　✧　✧

*R*EST, LIAM TOLD me.

He's right about a lot of things. Maybe he's right about this. I climb onto the cool pink sheets, hoping that a nap will suddenly make me content with this quiet little life.

Even though I know it won't.

Besides, I'm too wired to actually sleep. The white lace coverlet is both delicate and comfy. It's actually what I would have picked out for myself, except I didn't pick it out. I've been incapable of picking anything, of choosing anything, of deciding anything as part of some deep-seated fear that I'll be abandoned.

The coverlet, like everything else in my life, simply appeared.

And the person responsible for its appearance? Liam North.

I climb under the blanket and stare at the ceiling. My body feels overly warm, but it still feels good to be tucked into the blankets. The blankets *he* picked out for me.

It's really so wrong to think of him in a sexual way. He's my guardian, literally. Legally. And he has never done anything to make me think he sees *me* in a sexual way.

This is it. This is the answer.

I don't need to go skinny-dipping in the lake down the hill. Thinking about Liam North in a sexual way is my fast car. My parachute out of a plane.

My eyes squeeze shut.

That's all it takes to see Liam's stern expression, those fathomless green eyes and the glint of dark blond whiskers that are always there by late afternoon. And then there's the way he touched me. My forehead, sure, but it's more than he's done before. That broad palm on my sensitive skin.

My thighs press together. They want something between them, and I give them a pillow. Even the way I masturbate is small and timid, never making a sound, barely moving at all, but I can't change it now. I can't moan or throw back my head even for the sake of rebellion.

But I can push my hips against the pillow, rocking my whole body as I imagine Liam doing more than touching my forehead. He would trail his hand down my cheek, my neck, my shoulder.

Repressed. I'm so repressed it's hard to imagine more than that.

I make myself do it, make myself trail my

hand down between my breasts, where it's warm and velvety soft, where I imagine Liam would know exactly how to touch me.

You're so beautiful, he would say. *Your breasts are perfect.*

Because Imaginary Liam wouldn't care about big breasts. He would like them small and soft with pale nipples. That would be the absolute perfect pair of breasts for him.

And he would probably do something obscene and rude. Like lick them.

My hips press against the pillow, almost pushing it down to the mattress, rocking and rocking. There's not anything sexy or graceful about what I'm doing. It's pure instinct. Pure need.

The beginning of a climax wraps itself around me. Claws sink into my skin. There's almost certain death, and I'm fighting, fighting, fighting for it with the pillow clenched hard.

"Oh fuck."

The words come soft enough someone else might not hear them. They're more exhalation of breath, the consonants a faint break in the sound. I have excellent hearing. Ridiculous, crazy good hearing that had me tuning instruments before I could ride a bike.

My eyes snap open, and there's Liam, standing there, frozen. Those green eyes locked on mine. His body clenched tight only three feet away from me. He doesn't come closer, but he doesn't leave.

Orgasm breaks me apart, and I cry out in surprise and denial and relief. "*Liam.*"

It goes on and on, the terrible pleasure of it. The wrenching embarrassment of coming while looking into the eyes of the man who raised me for the past six years.

My hips pump against the mattress, pulling out the last few pulses between my legs.

And then I'm lying there, wrapped tight around a pillow, unable to move, panting.

I've never seen Liam looking anything other than calm and cool and capable. He can handle anything with a command that's almost terrifying in its competency. Right now he looks at a loss.

His voice is low and rough. "We should talk about this."

I can't think of anything in the world I'd rather do less. "Or we could just…" I hate that I still somehow sound breathy and turned on. There are little quivers in my thighs. "Pretend this never happened?"

"Come downstairs when you're—"

The sentence hangs between us, leaving me to

fill in the blank. *Come downstairs when you're done fucking yourself in the bed I bought for you. Come downstairs when you're done humiliating yourself.*

He gives a short nod, as if the unspoken answer is the right one.

Then he turns, an about-face appropriate to any military ceremony.

Alone in the room I have no choice but to face the mechanics of untangling myself. Unclenching my fists from the pillow. Pulling apart my legs. Acknowledging the dampness between my thighs.

"Please be a dream," I whisper, but my face is too hot. Burning up. This is real.

Want to read more? Overture is available on Amazon, iBooks, Barnes & Noble, and other book retailers!

Books by Skye Warren

Endgame Trilogy & more books in Tanglewood

The Pawn

The Knight

The Castle

The King

The Queen

Escort

Survival of the Richest

The Evolution of Man

The Bishop

Mating Theory

North Security Trilogy & more North brothers

Overture

Concerto

Sonata

Audition

Chicago Underground series

Rough

Hard

Fierce

Wild

Dirty

Secret

Sweet

Deep

Stripped series

Tough Love

Love the Way You Lie

Better When It Hurts

Even Better

Pretty When You Cry

Caught for Christmas

Hold You Against Me

To the Ends of the Earth

Standalone Dangerous Romance

Wanderlust

On the Way Home

Hear Me

For a complete listing of Skye Warren books, visit

www.skyewarren.com/books

About the Author

Skye Warren is the New York Times bestselling author of dangerous romance such as the Endgame trilogy. Her books have been featured in Jezebel, Buzzfeed, USA Today Happily Ever After, Glamour, and Elle Magazine. She makes her home in Texas with her loving family, sweet dogs, and evil cat.

Sign up for Skye's newsletter:
www.skyewarren.com/newsletter

Like Skye Warren on Facebook:
facebook.com/skyewarren

Join Skye Warren's Dark Room reader group:
skyewarren.com/darkroom

Follow Skye Warren on Instagram:
instagram.com/skyewarrenbooks

Visit Skye's website for her current booklist:
www.skyewarren.com

COPYRIGHT